QUICKFIC
ANTHOLOGY 2
Shorter-Short Speculative Fiction

By Digital Fiction

QUICKFIC
ANTHOLOGY 2
Shorter-Short Speculative Fiction

By Digital Fiction

DIGITAL SCIENCE FICTION | DIGITAL FANTASY FICTION | DIGITAL HORROR FICTION

DIGITAL FICTION
P U B L I S H I N G   C O R P

Collection copyright © 2016 Digital Fiction Publishing Corp.
Individual stories copyright © 2016 the Author
All rights reserved.

ISBN-13 (paperback): 978-1-927598-39-9
ISBN-13 (e-book): 978-1-927598-40-5

Table of Contents

Tough Crowd by Holly Schofield [sci-fi] 1
Reset by Eddie D. Moore [sci-fi] 5
Autumn Waits by Ken MacGregor [fantasy] 7
Watch Out for the Megafauna by Brenda Anderson [fantasy] 9
Someone Else by Jon Gauthier [horror] 13
Time Travelers Anonymous by Wendy Nikel [sci-fi] 17
She Dies by Jason Lairamore [sci-fi] 21
Shadow Can by Aeryn Rudel [horror] 31
Hubert and the Crone by S.C. Hayden [fantasy] 33
Next! by Preston Dennett [sci-fi] 39
Glass Future by Deborah Walker [sci-fi] 41
A Mary Shelley Moment by H.L. Fullerton [horror] 45
The Mother of Sands by Stewart C. Baker [horror] 47
First Date by Doree Weller [horror] 57
Dragon Dance by H.A. Titus [fantasy] 67
Copy That by Holly Schofield [sci-fi] 71
The Silver Witch by Tara Calaby [fantasy] 75
Born to It by Tara Calaby [fantasy] 79
Transition by Fred Waiss [fantasy] 85
As the Crow Flies by C.M. Saunders [horror] 93
Yard Sell by Karin Fuller [horror] 97
Spruce by Kolin Gates [horror] 107
Peach Cobbler by Lisa Finch [horror] 115
The Seeds of Foundation by Pedro Iniguez [sci-fi] 119
Old-Fashioned by H. A. Titus [sci-fi] 123
And Now, Fill Her In by Jamie Gilman Kress [fantasy] 127
The Gravedigger by Liam Hogan [horror] 133
How Earth Narrowly Escaped an Invasion from Space by Alex Shvartsman [sci-fi] 139
Hard to Swallow by Nick Nafpliotis [horror] 143

Table of Contents

The End of the World is, Like, So Boring by Amy Sisson [sci-fi] 149
Peppermint Tea in Electronic Limbo by DJ Cockburn [sci-fi] 155
Little More than Shadows by Stewart C. Baker [sci-fi] 165
Masks by Stewart C. Baker [sci-fi] 167
Lost Souls by E.E. King [horror] 175
Dear R.A.Y. by Tanya Bryan [sci-fi] 179
Death: A List by Tanya Bryan [horror] 181
The Key by Ian Whates [sci-fi] 185
You Could Count on That by David M. Hoenig [sci-fi] 189
You Did This by M.J. Sydney [horror] 195
The Princess's Kiss by Chuck Rothman [fantasy] 197
On a Clear Day You Can See All the Way to Conspiracy by Desmond Warzel [sci-fi] 203
Afternoon Break by Gregg Chamberlain [sci-fi] 215
The Monster In Me by Suzie Lockhart/ Bruce Lockhart 2nd [horror] 217
Spare Change by Chuck Rothman [fantasy] 225
Copyright 233

Tough Crowd by Holly Schofield [sci-fi]

"Hey, Ship? How about this one: A skeleton walks into a bar and says, 'Give me a beer and a mop.'"

I followed it with a "Ba-dum, tish," to indicate the end of the joke. No response. No surprise. It's hard to tell good jokes. It's even harder when you're the only human left on a deserted colony ship.

I'd been toying with the idea of a radio show back when Ship's corridors still rang with voices. I didn't begin broadcasting over Ship's comm until after the virus had turned my friends and fellow colonists into human jerky: dried husks; awful gaping mouths with their gums pulled back.

"Hey Ship, try saying 'gullible' really slowly. It sounds like 'oranges'."

"Phonetic interpretation makes it clear there is no correlation, sir."

"Just try saying it? Please?"

We'd probably picked up the virus at a rundown refueling port out Antares way. It acted fast. Two days later, I stumbled over a sobbing lieutenant in the mess hall. He died in my arms as I cursed the cheap, inconsistent immunizations the corporation had given us. Within hours, there were bodies in every room on Ship. I huddled by a comm crying out for anyone. Only Ship answered.

It took me two years to haul all three thousand bodies to the airlocks. The desiccating effect meant the smell wasn't too bad after the first month. As far as Ship could diagnose, the virus was a Vitamin K inhibitor. The fancy explanation was pseudohydroxycoumarin.

The simple explanation was that it worked like rat poison.

"Hey, Ship, light travels faster than sound, right?"

"That is correct, sir."

"So that's why some people appear bright until you hear them speak."

"I believe you are making a play on words involving the word 'bright'."

"Never mind, Ship."

I combed old files, updated ancient humor, wrote my own material, anything to have fresh jokes on my show. Anything to keep from thinking about the immense blackness outside, pressing against the hull. With Ship as my sole audience, I broadcast all types of comedy: stand-up, pranks, puns, verbal slapstick, limericks. I did it all.

Ship never laughed.

"Hey, Ship. Here's a maxim for you: An astronaut does not need a suit to evac. He only needs one to evac twice."

"This appears to be an example of dark humor. You have told me variations of this joke three times before." A pause. "It almost works."

Today, I gnawed on my apple and dropped the core where I finished it. A tiny cleaning bot, one of many, scooted around my foot and grabbed it seconds later. Keeping Ship tidy was not a problem. Fresh food, especially fruit from the hydroponics system, was not a problem. Deteriorating electronics, now *there* was a problem.

"Thruster failure on port side, sir," Ship intoned.

"Ship, I've told you many times. I do not want to see or hear about our journey or our hardware issues."

Especially since the navigation programs had failed and we were drifting aimlessly.

"Very well, sir. I will reset the reminder for three days from now."

I sucked in a deep breath in order to make an angry retort.

"Heh," said Ship.

I saw the telltale light flashing just as a voice spoke.

"Ahoy, this is Raven Six. Is anyone there?"

The voice from the other ship was loud and confident, and alive.

"Hello! Hello! I'm here!" I pressed the comm button so hard, my thumb turned white.

No response. No light on the comm panel.

"Ship! Open a channel to the other vessel! Now!"

"Open?" said Ship. "Open-faced sandwich? Open source? Open mike night?" It chuckled.

I tore the plastic sheeting off the nearest portscreen.

"Portscreen, enlarge and track!"

The other ship came into focus, receding as I watched. Soon it would be gone into the darkness of space.

"Ship, for the love of God! Let me talk to them!"

"Talk? Tick Tock? What does a chronometer do when it's hungry? It goes back four seconds!" Ship gave a mechanical guffaw.

I slumped against the wall below the comm panel. "Please," I whispered.

"Ahoy, do you read?" The voice from the other ship repeated, so human.

Human enough to leave the channel open. I heard him order, "Ensign, there's no response. Best to let it be. Might have K Virus. Back on course, full speed ahead."

Maybe I could race after them in the tiny transport shuttle. Staggering but not beaten yet, I angled across the room and slammed open the long horizontal handle on the seldom-used door. Ship, chortling, said something about walking into a heavy metal bar.

I charged down the corridor toward the shuttle bay. Dozens of cleaning bots scuttled out of my way as I turned the corner. I smelled fruit.

That's when I slipped on the first of many banana peels, strewn down the corridor like happy, yellow smiles.

Reset by Eddie D. Moore [sci-fi]

"Good morning Mr. Moss. Please don't get out of bed yet. The procedure was a complete success and you will be transferred to the training and readjustment center this afternoon."

"What happened? Who are you?"

"I'm sorry. I am Dr. Talbot. You are at the Whiteville Correctional facility in Salem, Oregon. I don't usually introduce people to their new life but we are a bit short handed, with the recent budget cuts."

"Why am I at a correctional facility? I cannot remember anything."

"Mr. Moss, I cannot tell you any details about your past. Your reintegration into society will have a greater chance of success if you don't know why you were treated."

"Treated? I don't understand."

"A large part of whom and what we are is determined by our past experiences. For most people, the elimination of a few memories will correct most of their social maladjustments. You, on the other hand, are a special case and were given a complete reset."

"What did I do?"

"Please. Don't fixate on the past. You have been given a blank slate, a new life, a fresh start without the hindrances of the past. Here, look over this pamphlet. There are some great career opportunities you can choose from."

"But I want to know who I am! What did I do to deserve this?"

"Mr. Moss, please take a deep breath. This will help you relax. The person you were no longer exists. I need you to focus on the future."

"I am focusing on the future! You just can't reset people like a computer!"

"This procedure has been performed hundreds of thousands of times over the last few years and our success rate is remarkably high. Honestly, it is more like restoring a computer to factory settings. Please lay back down! Nurse, help me restrain Mr. Moss."

"I will not be treated this way! Do you hear me? Let me go!"

"Mr. Moss, you are only making this worse by fighting it."

"Get that needle away from me I will not consent to any treatments!"

"Your treatment was court ordered, Mr. Moss. You cannot refuse it. There. That is better. Just relax."

"Nurse, keep Mr. Moss sedated. I will send an orderly after him shortly. I will just have to erase the last few minutes and try again."

"Yes Doctor, but I could have told you that the truth never works."

"Yes. Yes, you could have."

"Good morning Mr. Moss. I am Dr. Talbot. How are you feeling today?

"My head hurts. Where am I?"

"You are in the hospital. You took a hard hit on the head. What was the last thing you remember?"

"Nothing, I remember nothing."

"You have a unique case of amnestic syndrome, otherwise known as amnesia. You can see here on the scan the area of your brain that was damaged. I am sorry to inform you that there is only a small chance of your memory returning. The good news is that people with this condition, do go on to live full and productive lives."

"What do you know of my life?"

"I'm sorry Mr. Moss, I'm just a doctor. Look over this pamphlet. This facility specializes in cases like yours and the people there will be much more qualified to answer your questions. I will see that you are transferred this afternoon."

"Thank you doctor; I appreciate everything you have done for me. You have been very helpful."

"It was my pleasure, Mr. Moss. Have a great day."

Autumn Waits by Ken MacGregor [fantasy]

Autumn is tired. Her long hair, which had been green, then red and yellow and finally brown has begun to fall out. Her dress is tattered and her skin dry. She wants nothing more than to sleep. But, it is not yet time. So, she waits.

She thinks back over the last few months: the crisp, clear air; the bright skies; the apple cider; the children dressing up as pirates and monsters and eating too much candy. A sad smile plays across her lips.

Finally, Autumn sees Jack on the horizon. He's walking toward her, but taking his time. At this distance, he doesn't really seem to be getting any closer. She wishes he would hurry. She can barely keep her eyes open.

Jack struts, cocksure, his footsteps crunching the stiff grass. The prints Jack leaves behind are crushed brown grass tinged with white. He seems to take forever to cross the field to where Autumn sits. Every year, Jack comes to her, and every year, Autumn is ready to go; her very bones ache with the need for rest.

Finally, he is there. Jack looks into Autumn's eyes. She smiles at him. Seeing him here, now gives her comfort. This is as it should be.

"Hello, Mr. Frost," she says.

"My beautiful Autumn."

"Hard to believe," Autumn says, "it's already been a year."

"I know, love," Jack smiles at her. "I know."

Jack embraces Autumn and holds her close. He brushes a strand of hair from her brow and it falls to the ground. She can feel his cold touch long after it is gone. With a tenderness Autumn finds surprising every time, Jack kisses her. Autumn's life bleeds away with her warmth. Her awareness fades, and Autumn's last thought is a happy one. Finally, she can rest.

Jack lays her lifeless body on the ground. He always wishes he had more time with Autumn; he misses her already, but there is much to do. Besides, he will see her next year. She's always waiting for him. And, in a few months' time, he will see April. Bright, effusive April with her golden hair and sunshine smile. He's always anxious to see her by the end. By then, he too will be tired, and ready to sleep.

Watch Out for the Megafauna by Brenda Anderson [fantasy]

The long train slid across the West Australian desert. In the seat beside Bert, a sleeping man shifted position. A sheet of paper slipped from the man's lap to the floor. Bert reached for it, but his neighbor's hand closed on the paper, produced a pen and wrote:

'Wirth's Circus, coming soon to a window near you.'

Bert looked at his neighbor. The sleeping man's eyes remained closed. His chest rose and fell slowly. Some sort of trick, maybe? Bert looked out of the otherwise empty carriage. Telephone poles ran parallel to the train line. The clear blue sky was as empty as the desert. Bert looked back. The words *'Someone always dies'* now trailed across the paper.

The sleeping man slumped sideways. Bert leapt up. A passing attendant sprinted past him, leaping over seats to get to the window. Outside, a colossal kangaroo thumped into sight, jumped, sailed right over the telephone wires and landed, *thunk*, on the other side.

Other attendants rushed to the window. Bert elbowed his way between them.

"Wow, *Macropus titan*," said one attendant, with awe. "I can never get over these giant kangaroos. Think the Mihirung will put in an appearance?"

"Giant flightless birds aren't famous for their acrobatic skills," said one. "But, you never know."

Bert cleared his throat. "Er, my neighbor back there seems to have fainted."

The attendants nodded, eyes glued to the window. "Yeah. It happens."

Bert peered out the window. "Is this a projection or something? Some type of entertainment?"

"Are you kidding?" said one.

"If these guys turn up," said another, "it's always round about here, half way across the Nullarbor. Look!"

A massive marsupial with enormously strong forelimbs padded forward like an outsize lion. An even more massive giant emu followed. A smaller giant bird with longer legs leapt forward, bounced up onto the lion's back and sailed up into the air, landing with ease on the telephone lines. It ducked its head and took short, mincing steps forward.

All the attendants cheered.

"*Dromornis stirtoni*," said one. "Giant demon duck of death. Look at that! I've seen it. I believe it."

"Wow," said the other. "Megafauna and demon ducks. It just doesn't get any better."

The funambulist emu ducked its head as if acknowledging their applause.

Inside the train carriage, a sudden high pitched scream made everyone turn round. A passenger hyperventilated and pointed at Bert's slumped neighbor. Attendants left the window and rushed up. A uniformed employee touched the man's neck and looked solemn.

The official turned to Bert. "This is your seat, sir?"

Bert nodded.

"Your neighbor's dead," said the official.

Bert said nothing.

"What were you doing? Enjoying the scenery?" said the official.

Bert looked out the window. The megafauna had vanished. Now only featureless desert slid past the windows.

"Sorry," Bert said.

The official bent down and picked up the sheet of paper from the floor.

"I never get used to it, myself," said the official, studying the paper. "There's always a note, you see. Odd, really. Automatic writing used to be popular, centuries back. An old parlor room trick. The subject could be comatose but his fingers still wrote some message or other. I guess that's what stands out with this Circus. They've dug out all the oldies."

"Oldies? Circus? You mean you know about those animals?" said Bert.

The official nodded. "We don't like to advertise, though. Too random. Every now and then a passenger sees something and probably puts it down to stress, or alcohol. Very popular, those items."

"But," Bert said, even more confused. "I saw them. They were huge. Mega big kangaroos and emus and something else built like a tank …"

"That would be the *Thylacoleo carnifex*," said the official. "Commonly called marsupial lions. Absolutely massive muscle power. The Circus sure loves the shock factor."

"Circus? You said that before. How, by any stretch of definition or imagination, could this be called a circus?" said Bert, wide-eyed.

The official looked down at the sheet of paper. "Yeah, well, we've done some research, believe me. Best we can figure, in the 1900's something called Wirth's Circus toured rural Australia. Animals, tightrope walkers, a magician, someone doing automatic writing, the usual stuff. Nothing special." He paused. "There's no record of what happened next, or why that circus turns up here, much later, half way across the Nullarbor, mixing time and megafauna circus acts. All we know is that it happens at roughly this point on the Nullarbor Plain. Sometimes I wonder if it's a type of afterimage, but all mixed up. Massive, extinct animals doing aerial tricks. One thing in the program never changes, though. The guy who does the automatic writing always dies."

Bert stared at him.

"Always?"

The official nodded. "Always."

"I've never actually seen anyone die before," said Bert.

"Yeah, well." The official turned to his colleagues. "Guess no-one got a photo?"

The attendants shook their heads.

The official pulled a face. "One day we'll get lucky."

Bert took himself to the dining carriage and stayed with a bottle of scotch for the rest of the day. When he returned to his seat, all trace of his dead neighbor had vanished.

Years passed. Whenever business took him to Perth, Bert opted to fly rather than take the train. One day on a plane cruising at 550 mph, focused on nothing but his laptop screen, he passed over the same section of the Nullarbor Plain.

It was quiet. Too quiet. He looked up. All the seats were empty. Everyone crowded round the windows. Bert opened the blind on his window just as a massive kangaroo leaped over the plane's wing.

On his laptop his slackening fingers tapped words. Bert felt his heart slow down and as the laptop slid from his lap, he made out the words:

'We've got trampolines.'

Someone Else by Jon Gauthier [horror]

Basil watched Janet as she paced up and down the room, rubbing her hands together in that irritating way that only she could.

"It can't do you any good to worry," Basil said, remaining perfectly at ease in the leather lounger. Janet ignored him and continued her journey. Basil watched curiously. Part of him—the part that still adored her after nearly 50 years of marriage—actually felt slightly bad.

"Why don't you just sit down?" he said. "You're going to give yourself an attack."

As if obeying him, Janet immediately stopped walking and spun around to face the leather lounger. Then her eyes darted about as if she was searching for a bird that had made its way into the room.

"There's someone else in here," she said. She said it so seriously, so matter-of-factly, that it was impossible to not believe her.

"You're imagining things," Basil said, not trying at all to hide the condescension in his voice. "After all these years, you've finally gone batty."

Without replying, Janet moved to the other side of the room so she was only a couple of feet from him.

"I think it's a ghost," she said. Her eyes were on the ceiling now. Basil sighed and got to his feet.

"Don't be ridiculous, dear. You know there's no such thing."

Janet walked towards the casket and looked at the body inside. She squinted slightly as if trying to work out a great mystery in her head.

"It would make sense, you know," she said. Her voice infused with thoughtfulness. "They probably all come to these places. Trying to get one last look at themselves before they're sealed in these wooden cells. Trying to see which friends and family members actually had the decency to show up at their funerals." She continued to observe the corpse, studying its perfectly pressed outfit and its rose colored cheeks.

"Why would you color a dead person's cheeks?" she asked. "What exactly is the point?"

Basil walked up behind his wife and placed a hand on her shoulder. "Come on, dear," he said softly. "No sense in upsetting yourself."

Suddenly, Janet spun around, her eyes still squinted into mystery-solving mode.

"There *is* a ghost in here," she exclaimed. "I just know it." With that, she made her way past Basil and towards the coat closet. As she flung it open, Basil could hear her muttering to herself in that… that way. That way she muttered to herself all the time.

It had started as soon as he got back from Vietnam. They'd only been married a year when he got drafted. He had left her as a strong and joyful young man and returned with a shredded lower spine and a head full of horrors. Bound to a wheelchair, Basil was forced to watch his young and bright-eyed wife age into a bitter and resentful hag. He couldn't give her children or any kind of life he had promised. She was nothing but a nursemaid to a broken vet—a role that she accepted because it was her Christian duty.

"Just tell me what you want!" Janet cried. "Why are you here?"

"Give it up," Basil said. "There's no one listening."

Janet made her way towards the casket again and tilted her eyes to the thing inside.

"Is it you?" she asked. The corpse didn't respond.

"Now you're just being ridiculous," Basil said with a scoff. "Actually talking to a dead body. What if someone were to come in here and see you acting like this?"

Janet placed her palms on the casket and hung her head. Basil could see tears starting to fall from her eyes.

"So there is still some heart in you after all," he said.

"Just leave me alone," Janet whispered. "I've put up with you for half a century. I just want some peace and quiet."

Basil let out a sigh and moved towards her.

"Do you remember it, dear?" he asked softly. He was beside her now, almost whispering into her ear: "Do you remember how it felt? To feel a life extinguished right in front of you—to feel a heartbeat actually stop."

Basil saw a chill take hold of her and creep downward, each part of her body shuddering as it slunk across. She didn't respond. She just stared down at the man in the casket, her face expressionless.

"I saw such terrible things over there," Basil said. "It was indescribable. I'm sorry it had to come between us." He put his hand on hers—and for a moment, he thought he could actually feel her skin.

"I remember these hands," he whispered. "They were so cold on my throat. So much hatred in these hands."

Janet suddenly let out a gasp and buckled over, the tears flowing freely now. Basil could see the goose bumps on her arms. He felt his mouth bend into a smile.

"Don't be upset, dear," Basil said, stealing a glance at his pale body. "I'm not going anywhere."

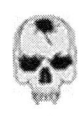

Time Travelers Anonymous by Wendy Nikel [sci-fi]

"Hi, my name is Jen, and I'm addicted to time travel."

"Hi, Jen," the somber group intoned. A few made eye contact, but most continued to stare at their feet. A girl in a baseball cap across the room picked at her nails, poorly hidden headphone cords snaking their way down her neck and into her purse.

"Jen, why don't you tell us about your experience, and when you first knew you had a problem?"

"Well, I was born twenty years ago, but as you can tell by the stubborn wrinkles and gray hairs, I've spent quite a bit of time traveling as well. Last I calculated, I think I've lived out about forty-five or fifty years."

A few heads nodded. A few nervous hands tugged at their own gray hairs and brushed across the premature wrinkles that no expensive anti-aging cream would diminish.

"I started way back in high school. At first, it was just a quick research trip here or there, but then a friend showed me how I could use it to lengthen my weekends. I'd leave Friday after work, and to everyone else it seemed that I'd had a normal two-day weekend, but I'd really spent a week taking in the Chicago World's Fair or drinking at a speakeasy—"

"Yeah, partyin' with Gatsby." A man across the room winked and nodded knowingly.

"Let's keep this on topic, Raúl. Go on, Jen."

"Eventually, my schoolwork started suffering. I'd excuse myself to use the washroom during class and go spend a month or two out in gold rush era California, or hanging out with my grandma during her wild teen years. Sometimes I'd just go back to my own childhood and rewatch my favorite cartoons. Cartoons were so much better back then."

Around the room, heads nodded.

"Anyway, by the time I got back to school, I wouldn't remember a thing about the lecture. I once spent six months pretending to be a Southern Belle in Antebellum Mississippi, and when I came back, I'd completely forgotten that I was supposed to be on a date with my boyfriend. I walked right past him and out of the restaurant. Ten minutes later he sent me a break-up text. I couldn't even remember how to use the stupid cell phone to text him back."

"Was that the moment of your revelation?"

"I... I'm not sure what you mean."

"Well, is there anyone else here that would be willing to share with Jen the story of your own revelation, the moment when you realized you had a problem?" A few hands slowly crept toward the ceiling. "Ivan, go ahead, why don't you tell your story?"

"Yo. Name's Ivan. So, the first time I knew, like, for sure that I had a problem was when I met a chick at a concert — real nice girl, big hair, loud laugh — anyway, I asked her out, but when I went to pick her up, I had to wait for her in her mama's front hallway and there, right on the wall, was an old-timey picture of a girl I'd gone out with on one of my trips to the past. Turns out my new girlfriend was my old girlfriend's granddaughter. I turned around and ran — and I mean *ran* — straight to this here community center to see when the next one of these meetings was gonna be."

A few people clapped, but most just shifted awkwardly in their seats.

"Anyone else? Go ahead, Thalia."

"Well, I first knew I had a problem when I ended up in one of those paradoxes—"

Around the circle, people nodded and chuckled.

"Yeah, you know what I mean? I'm sure I'm not the only one it's happened to, but man, it messes with you. Anyway, this was one of those weird ones where I made the stupid mistake of giving something to my past self. It was ridiculous, really, this dumb little rag doll, and the worst part of it was that it didn't even really mean anything. I mean, I *wish* it'd been some family heirloom or a winning lottery ticket or something... I don't know... *important*, but no, it was just this stupid, cheap doll that I'd played with as a kid. I never could remember where I'd gotten it; I just kind of figured it was from my mom or grandma or something, right?

"But one day I found it in my closet and it made me all nostalgic, so I went back to the old neighborhood where we used to live in before my parents divorced, and for whatever reason, I brought the stupid doll along. I don't even know why. I was just feeling sentimental, I guess. But as soon as I saw that little girl sitting on the front stoop, all by her lonesome, I just. . . I didn't even think about it. It just happened and there I was, handing her that stupid, ugly doll. And then I remembered. That's where I'd gotten it — from some stranger who'd happened to walk by when I was playing outside one day."

Thalia wiped her eyes. A box of Kleenex made its way around the room.

"It was kind of unnerving, you know? Makes you wonder what's real."

Heads bobbed. The girl in the baseball cap yawned.

"Thank you, Thalia. Anyone else? No one? Okay, Jen, back to you. Now that you've had some time to think about it, do you know when you realized that you had a problem?"

"You know, to tell you the truth, I didn't think I had a problem. I only came here because my sister asked me to. She's older than me — well, biologically anyway. She hasn't traveled much, so she still looks ten or fifteen years younger than me now. Anyway, she said she was worried about me, and I promised her I'd come, but now that I'm here, I can see that she was right. I definitely have a problem."

"Well, we're very glad that we were able to convince you of that. Was there something in particular that spoke to you? One of the others' stories, perhaps?"

"No. Actually, I just realized..." She pointed at the girl with the baseball cap tucked over her eyes. "I've been here before."

She Dies by Jason Lairamore [sci-fi]

The roar of the nearby monster hurt Missy Welton's ears and rattled the window above where she crouched. She gripped the pitiful feeling laser-gun she carried in both hands and cursed under her breath as she shimmied across the room to the door leading out to the cobbled street beyond.

She should have brought a more powerful weapon to battle the behemoth out there, but she hadn't wanted to be burdened by the added bulk, and besides, she needed to practice her precision shooting anyway.

Another building crumbled into rubble, this one cater-corner to where she peeked around the edge of the open door. The debris spewed out in a spray that rained down on the office building where she hid. The window she had just left exploded. Glass shot out and scored a shallow groove along her shoulder blade. Warm blood ran down her back, soiling the pretty flower dress she wore.

She winced at the sharp pain and gritted her teeth as she looked toward where the building had stood. A cloud of yellow dust billowed out from the site. Now was her chance. The monster had ruined her dress and that couldn't stand.

With the gun pointing out in front of her, she darted through the doorway and down the street toward the concealing fog. The creature roared again and she covered her ears. It was close, so close. If she could only get a clear line of sight, then she knew she could kill it.

At the corner of the street, she stopped and wedged herself against a couple of walls in the building opposite the ruin. She pointed her gun as the fog slowly cleared. There was movement. It looked like a shadowy building rocking from side to side. She trained her gun toward the top of the massive creature and waited for the air to show it clear.

The monster was white and shiny, like silver glass in a feathery pattern that covered its blocky body. Its arms were as broad as her dad's SUV and ended in sharp, diamond-looking claws. Her gun wouldn't do a thing to a body so heavily armored. It had to be an eye. She strained to make out the details of its head as the thing continued to swing its massive arms.

The building next to the one it had already destroyed crumbled into dust. Debris rained down as another yellow cloud erupted. She tried to find the things eyes, but couldn't. Its head was nothing but a solid block with a large opening in the middle for its screaming mouth.

She grunted as a falling brick clipped her leg, tearing her dress and raking the skin underneath. There were no eyes on its head. As she shifted her weight off her injured side, she quickly scanned the creature before the new debris fog engulfed it.

The monster had eyes on its belly. They were little orb-shaped pinpricks depressed in its silvery feathers. She took aim and fired as the yellow mist blew out over the scene.

A scream of pain so loud that it rattled her bones was her reward. With a smile, she lowered her weapon and turned her head toward the street leading away from the creature. It was sure to flail about now and she didn't want to be anywhere near while it underwent its death throes.

But her legs wouldn't move. She jerked her upper half, but it was no use. Her feet had frozen in place. A sharp crack from above alerted her of danger. Looking up, she saw a piece of the building she was beside break free. It was falling straight toward her. She leaned with all her might, but still didn't budge.

The world about her took on a washed out, gray tint as it began to fade. She looked up once more in time to see the chunk of building right before it crashed down on her.

She lay in a tumbled heap on the floor of her now clear-screened virtual reality orb. Everything hurt.

"Get unplugged from that contraption and come to the kitchen," her dad called. She came to hands and knees and tried to will away the pain she knew wasn't real.

"You let Jeff kill me Dad," she called out. Oh, how her little brother was sure to gloat. He had never killed her before on the battlefield.

"Kitchen, young lady," Dad said again and was gone from her room. She groaned at the lingering aches that covered her and got to her feet. Against one wall of the VR orb was a panel that placed and removed the adhesives patches it required up and down her spine. She leaned against the machine and it disconnected her from the system. After she was fully disengaged, the orb split open and she exited.

She dressed in her favorite flower dress, a white one with red roses, and headed to the kitchen to see what was so important as to interrupt her and Jeff's battle.

"I killed you!" her brother Jeff yelled the moment she entered the kitchen. Jeff had just turned nine years old. He had put on his t-shirt inside-out so that the seams showed at the shoulder. A grin covered his chubby face and his cheeks were red with excitement.

"Wait until I tell everyone at school that I killed a twelve-year-old!" he crooned.

"Dad unplugged me or I wouldn't have died," she said and stuck her tongue out at him.

"Nuh uh, Dad unplugged me too, but I still saw the kill on my tally bar before the session stopped."

"Missy, Jeff, quiet," Dad said. He and Mom were sitting at the kitchen table. Dad's jaw muscles were standing out and Mom's face was chalky white.

"What?" she asked in the tone she used when she was trying to be as serious as an adult. She could tell Dad was upset, but that wasn't all that unusual. He was always mad when she and Jeff played in the orb. Mom looked scared though, and that was new.

"Sit down," he said. She did so immediately. Jeff, oblivious to everything that wasn't directly related to what he cared about, skipped over with that stupid smile still on his face.

"I've enrolled us into colonization," Dad said.

She frowned at him and glanced at Mom, whose face seemed to have gotten even whiter.

"Colonization?" she asked, shaking her head. She'd seen the vids on the news apps that popped up on her social feed, same as everybody else, but had never paid them much mind. The people moving away to jungles and deserts on other planets and living like cave people were just ads that added color to all her friends' postings on her feed.

"That's right," Dad said. "We're getting away before all this tech rots your minds to mush and wastes your bodies to jelly."

He had said the words with the same edge to his voice that he always seemed to use lately.

Mom started to cry.

"People aren't meant to live this way Bea," Dad said to Mom in a softer voice.

"We're leaving Earth?" Jeff asked. His eyes were wide as he stared at Dad.

All Missy could think about was her friends online at school. Tom had asked to meet her in real life only yesterday. And she had a math test coming up later in the week. Then there was the virtual track meet this weekend. All of her friends were going to be there.

"Dad, we can't go," she said. He couldn't be serious. Their whole life was here. Everybody she knew was here, in VR.

Dad flexed his jaw muscles again as he nodded at her. "It's time you learned what real life is about."

Her body felt numb like it did every time she was shutting out of the net. She waited for the kitchen's cream colored walls to fade away, but they never did.

She shook her head slightly. "But –," she looked at Mom who was still crying and back to the hard, brown eyes of Dad.

"It's for your own good, Missy," he said. He looked over at Jeff. "And you too, Jeff. I want you guys to be strong, like people are supposed to be."

"I'll die if you make me go!" she yelled and jumped from her chair. She ran to her room so that she wouldn't have to see them anymore. It wasn't real. It couldn't be real.

She didn't even have time to say goodbye to her friends. Dad must have signed them up for the trip months ago, because no sooner had she shut her bedroom door and taken a step toward her VR orb, and he was there.

"We're leaving Missy," he said. "No need to pack. Everything has been taken care of."

She turned from the open door of her orb with every intention of squaring up to Dad and telling him that he could not make her go. She even went so far as to stick her chest out and lift her chin before her eyes met his. That was when her resolve crumbled. The look on Dad's face was made of stone. She knew that nothing she said would make the least bit of difference.

"I hate you," she said and ran past him through her open bedroom door.

Mom and Jeff were in the living room by the front door. Mom was no longer crying, but her shoulders were slumped.

"Mom, talk to him," she whispered. "Don't let him take us."

Mom wouldn't look her in the eye. She glanced to Jeff's chubby face and then looked down at the tiled floor.

"I agree with him, Miss. It'll be good for us."

Some small kernel of hope that she hadn't even known was there burnt to a cinder in her stomach.

"It might be fun, Missy," Jeff said.

What did he know.

They drove in silence through the busy streets of the light-filled metropolis, but she didn't see any of it. It was like how she felt when the VR was downloading whatever world she was entering. She floated in limbo and waited to see where she ended up materializing. When they reached the public spaceport, Dad ushered them through the lobby and then past the front desk lady. They were led up a steep set of steps into an oval room by a man wearing a white uniform and made to secure themselves into soft reclining chairs.

"Good luck," the man said and then he was gone.

She Dies

She didn't remember falling asleep, but she must have. She had a headache and her mouth was dry. Dad handed her a water bottle. She tried to focus her eyes on him, but they were all gummy and didn't want to open right.

"That water will fix you right up," he said. His voice, for the first time in what seemed like a long time, sounded excited.

"Where are we?" she croaked as she lifted the bottle to her lips.

"Our new home," he said.

Dad left and she drank the water, which did make her feel better. She got out of her chair and nearly fell down. She felt heavy.

"Gravity is a bit more than you're used to," Mom said, coming up beside her. Missy looked around at the other people with them and noticed that everybody else seemed to be having the same problem that she was having.

"Mom -," she began.

"Give it a try, okay Missy?" Mom asked, cutting her off.

She was going to ask Mom if she still thought this was a good idea, but she guessed that it didn't really matter now. They were here.

Missy descended the steep steps and the door slid open to show the world beyond. The sky was bright green and the sun was white! What looked like purple-leaved trees covered everything.

The ship had landed in what looked like burnt off land. The dirt was black and the smell of ash lay heavy on the air.

"Was there a fire?" She asked Dad, who had come up beside her.

He laid a hand on her shoulder. "That's just how this place smells, Miss."

"Come on, let's explore!" Jeff called and took off at a waddling jog away from the ship.

Dad laughed. "Go," he said and pushed her after Jeff. "Keep an eye on your brother."

There were squat, dull-gray buildings dotting the little area around the ship. She caught up to Jeff after passing the first circle of them.

"Jeff, wait," she said, pulling him to a stop.

The short run already had her brother breathing hard.

"I feel heavy," he said between gulps of ash-tinged air.

"You are heavy," she said with a wicked grin.

"Ha-ha."

She let her joke drop and looked around. "Jeff, remember the first rule of exploring?"

"Weapons!" he answered. "But what is there? It isn't like we have an inventory tab to choose from like back home."

The thought of the VR orb and her never being able to play it again made her chest ache, but she remembered Mom telling her to give this place a try. She frowned at the box-like buildings surround them.

"Maybe those are our inventory tabs," she said and pointed toward the closest building.

Jeff caught on to the idea right away. "Let's go see."

The buildings were little houses it turned out, with a bunch of inset machines used for cooking and cleaning. Even the beds were inset. They started opening all the little doors along the walls in search for something to use as weapons.

"Look!" Jeff called.

He had found a closet full of tools.

"Perfect," she said.

They argued over the best things and finally agreed that she should carry the machete and him the ax.

"Now we're ready," she said.

They left the house and continued in the direction away from the ship. After the second circular arrangement of houses, they saw what looked like a dull gray wall up ahead.

"What is that?" Jeff asked. She cursed under her breath as they got closer. No wonder Dad hadn't been concerned when they had run off to explore. The entire area was surrounded by a big metal wall.

"That's just great," she said as they reached the wall.

One of the purple-leaved trees had fallen against the wall. Its top hung over.

"Looks like we can't explore after all," she continued. She bent and picked up a clod of the black dirt and threw it at the purple treetop. Jeff followed her lead. Before long they were racing to see who could hit the tree hard enough to make some of its leaves fall off.

"A purple leaf can be our first badge of accomplishment!" Jeff yelled. He was out of breath again.

Just then, the whole treetop shook and a rain of leaves fell to the ground. Jeff, who had been a couple of steps in front of her, dropped his ax and raced ahead with a cry of glee.

A hiss followed and a large, dark-green, snakelike creature fell to the ground right in front of him.

"Jeff! Come back!"

The monster's head reminded her of a Venus flytrap. She instinctively tried to find its eyes, but she couldn't see any.

The monster snatched Jeff up. She was running toward him even as the creature was coiling its long body around Jeff's struggling form.

She threw the clod she still had in her hand at the thing and scored a hit right into its open mouth.

"Let him go!" she screamed.

The monster hissed at her and the smell of rotten eggs hit her in the face. She didn't stop running, though. As soon as she was close enough, she swung the machete.

Its head was too high for her to reach, so instead she aimed for the coils surrounding Jeff. A foul stench like when mom had boiled cabbage one time erupted when her blade bit into the thing's smooth, dark-green skin.

The creature jerked and threw Jeff away. Her eyes followed her brother's flight. She had time to worry that he might be hurt when an agonizing pressure crushed her left side. She was lifted from the ground as her breath squeezed out of her.

She turned her head and saw the head of the monster up close. Now she could see its eyes. They were three flat little slits on top of its head. She would have to remember that if she ever got her hands on a gun.

A gun! She still, somehow, held her machete in her right hand. She twisted in the thing's massive jaws and felt something rip. But she was nearly numb to the pain now. With everything she had, she swung the long knife at the things head.

Then she was falling.

She woke up groggy.

"Six broken ribs, three puncture wounds, and a collapsed lung," a voice said. "Lucky it didn't get her heart."

Mom was crying beside her. Dad was there too, and Jeff. Another man, the one that had spoken, talked again.

"I'll give you guys some privacy."

"Thanks," Dad said. The man nodded and left.

"I'm so sorry, sweetie," Dad said. "They put up those barriers to keep the natural wildlife out. It was a freak thing that allowed that thing access to the settlement."

She shook her head a little. "That's okay. Jeff, are you alright?"

Jeff nodded. His face was so white.

"The ship has a return mission in two weeks for those who've changed their minds. I've already told the captain we plan on being on it," Dad said. "I never should have brought us here. I'm so sorry, Miss."

She shook her head as he finished. What she had been through was so much better than any of the orb games she had played. There were monsters here, real monsters, and they could really kill. She had never actually thought of the difference that would make. It changed everything.

"I want to stay," she said. She didn't need VR here.

"But you almost died, for real this time!" Jeff blurted.

"But I didn't," she said and smiled. "I saved you." She had really saved him. That mattered so much more than doing it on a game.

Dad frowned. Mom ran a hand through her hair.

"We'll talk about it later," Mom said. "You just rest and get better."

She nodded then a thought struck her.

"Where's my flower dress?"

Dad half smiled. "Ruined, sweetie."

She wanted to laugh but even trying hurt too much. That couldn't stand.

Shadow Can by Aeryn Rudel [horror]

When I was little, I was afraid of my shadow. Mama told me I was right to be afraid. She said your shadow is a dark reflection, an almost-invisible demon bound to your fleshy self. She said it was a collection of all the ugly things about you, all the bad thoughts you don't act on but still think about. I grew up, and I stopped being afraid. I thought Mama was just spinning some of that Louisiana hoodoo she grew up with to scare us. I should have believed her.

It started one long July afternoon. I was lying on my bed, sweating like a bastard in the hot Georgia summer and wearing nothing but a pair of skivvies and my sweat-slicked skin. My shadow flickered and moved across the ceiling as the sun streamed into my tiny bedroom.

Maybe it was some kind of heat daze, or maybe it was the pot I'd smoked the night before with Tommy Nelson across the hall, but a strange thought occurred to me—I should tell my shadow to do something, to get me something I wanted. I pointed at the ceiling where my shadow hung like a cool spot of shade just out of reach and said, "Shadow, get me a Coke."

My shadow didn't do shit, and I remember laughing at the absurdity of the thing, turning over, and despite the murderous heat, falling asleep. When I woke up a few hours later, I saw a bottle of Coke sitting on my rickety old nightstand. It was the most beautiful and terrifying thing I'd ever seen.

The room had grown darker in the late afternoon, and the shadows had thickened. I saw *my* shadow against the far wall, opposite where it should be from how the light was coming in. It was waiting, unmoving, a blot of eager darkness on the white plaster. It's head—my head, I guess—moved a bit, a nod maybe. That was all it took.

Over the next couple of weeks, I learned what my shadow could do. It could bring me things and not just sodas from the liquor store. It could bring me the cash out of the liquor store's register. It could bring me that new pistol I wanted at the pawn shop. All I had to do was make sure there was enough light, and when my shadow was flung up against the wall, I just told it what to do. "Shadow, bring me this. Shadow, get me that."

I think acknowledging it for what it was made it free. Admitting it was something with a mind of its own was enough. The Wilsons' cat died first. His name was Ralph, and he sometimes came into my bedroom in the morning and slept on my bed. I liked that little fur ball. My shadow knew that. It knows everything about me. I found Ralph on the foot of my bed a week ago, still and ice cold. His eyes were black, like the life had been sucked right out of them. My shadow was on the wall across from my bed, watching. It wanted me to see what it had done.

I ran out of my apartment that day, sick and terrified. Stupid, really. How can you run from your own shadow? After Ralph, I stopped asking my shadow to do things. If I didn't ask for anything, maybe it didn't have the freedom to do what *it* wanted. I thought that until Tommy Nelson's baby died. They said it was crib death, but I overheard one of the EMTs when they took little Amanda away. The EMT looked scared, and she said the baby's eyes looked like black marbles.

Amanda died last night, and I called Mama this morning. She called me stupid. She called me foolish. But she said she'd come. Mama told me the truth when I was little; your shadow is all that's ugly about you, it's all the bad thoughts you think when you're mad. Amanda used to cry at night and wake me up. Ralph pissed on my bed once. Amanda and Ralph made me angry, made me think terrible things I would never do. My shadow remembered those things; it probably remembers a lot more.

I think it still needs me to get into this world, and if Mama can't fix this, then I'll drive out to the old quarry off Route 23. The pond there is three hundred feet deep. I'll bet that far down there are no shadows.

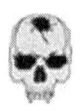

Hubert and the Crone by S.C. Hayden [fantasy]

"Can you make my lips rosy red," the crone asked. "Can you make my skin creamy soft, my bosom plump, my thighs firm, my nest hot and tight?"

The wicker nodded.

"Course you can, course you can." The crone smiled wet and gummy. "And would you? Would you make me all these things and more? Would you do it for me, Bloody Robin, Black Sam, Wicker Man, King?"

The wicker did not move.

"Would you do it for a blood sacrifice?"

Slowly, the wicker nodded.

The crone ran a bony hand over the killing table, traced the tabletop's deep runnels with her finger. "So say you," she whispered.

She'd made the wicker weeks before, fashioned him from sticks and twine, muttering strange old words all the while. She'd filled his sackcloth head with ashes, peat, and yew seeds, given him black button eyes and stitched a silent zigzag mouth. She'd sealed him lovingly with tar and pitch and hardened him with smoke.

When he was ready, she placed a black dog's heart in his chest and waited. The wind wailed and the bone moon gleamed. The crone rocked and hummed and when the hour was right, she sang.

It took longer than it had when she'd done it last, three hundred years ago, but before her song was through, the black dog's dead heart thumped.

Hubert woke to the smell of baked bread. He hadn't eaten in over a week and his stomach clenched, but he knew the crone wouldn't give him any. Cripple yes, but not stupid. He knew what the old woman was and what was to become of him. "Blood sacrifice," she'd called him. She wasn't subtle.

With his true leg, Hubert pushed himself to the rear of the cage. His gimp leg dragged twisted, withered and useless. He rolled to his side and pissed in a pile of woodchips. The crone hadn't even given him a bucket.

Hubert's cage was made of ash wood, each bar thick as his wrist. If that wasn't enough, he wore an iron collar, fixed to an iron chain, fixed to an iron ball as thick as his head.

"Thirsty?" the crone said.

Hubert rolled away from the piss soaked chips and slithered to the front of the cage. The crone was peering in at him, eyes bright and hungry.

"Yes," he said. "But I'd rather have some of that bread I smell."

"Ha!" The crone laughed. "I bet you would. Nine days you haven't eaten. A nine-day fast purifies a man, or boy, as the case may be. Pure, pure, pure; a proper meal for Black Sam."

The crone slid a bowl of water through the bars. Hubert snatched it up and drank, hating himself more with every swallow.

"Would you believe me if I told you I was once the prettiest creature in the valley?" The crone said, running a liver spotted hand through her thin white hair. "Oh, the lads would come from far and wide for a chance to play with me. And play with them I did, but not always how they wanted."

"You're still beautiful," Hubert said. "The loveliest I've laid eyes on."

"Ha!" The crone threw her head back and laughed. "Do you say so? And I suppose you'd take me to bed? Whisper honey in my ear? A nice pump and tickle, then choke me in my sleep?"

"No," Hubert said. "I wouldn't."

"I should open your belly for you. Feed you to my pigs. Be done with it. A blood sacrifice is too good an end. Lucky for you, Black Sam isn't picky."

Hubert felt his eyes burn red. He didn't want to break down. He didn't want to cry, but the tears came anyway. *Weak, weak, weak*, he thought, shaking his head.

"Now, now," the crone said, "don't cry, wee one. It'll all be over soon. No more suffering. Besides, there are far worse things than death."

"I'm not afraid to die," Hubert said. "In fact, I want to. You don't know what it's like to be a weakling. To be an orphan, a cripple."

The crone regarded Hubert in silence. A thoughtful look settled her brow.

"Those who go willing make the best offerings. I can make it quick, so I can."

"How?"

"Just say it. Just offer yourself to me. Offer yourself to Bloody Robin."

"What would become of me, *after*?"

"Even such as me can't say for sure. But there are some who believe that those who go willing gain power in the next world. Would you like that, wee one? Would you like Black Sam to make you strong in the world to come?"

"I would."

"Say it then."

Hubert paused, but not for very long. "I offer myself to you."

"Yes, wee one, almost there. To me and who else?"

"Bloody Robin, Black Sam, Wicker Man, King."

The crone's face twisted. She bent over backwards and scuttled crabwise across the floor. Green smoke billowed from her nose and from her mouth. Yowling and wailing like a cat in heat, she thrashed and shook, then collapsed in a heap.

The crone did not move. As the hours slid past, Hubert thought he'd somehow killed her, but when the sun fell and the window darkened, she rose.

"Time, time, time," she said, "time to see the wicker."

With a twist of her hand, the cage door opened and the chain fell away from Hubert's neck.

"Come my pet, my wee little darling, my honey bunny boy. Come, come, come."

Hubert slithered out of the cage, rolled onto his back and stared up at the crone from the floor.

"How will I walk?" Hubert said. "You broke my crutches when you took me from the foundling's home. Broke them and burned them."

"So I did, wee one, so I did."

The crone raised her arm and a long gnarled walking stick shot into the air as though it had been held underwater, then released. It floated across the room and came to rest in her outstretched hand.

Slowly, painfully, Hubert pulled himself up with the proffered staff. He hadn't stood in nine days and his back sang. When he was on his feet, one planted strong and one curled and twisted, his vision dimmed and his head swam. For a moment, Hubert thought he would hit the floor, but he rallied.

"Follow me," the crone said.

Hubert followed through an archway and into a section of the house he hadn't been able to see from his cage. On the far side of the room, like some profane scarecrow king, a wicker man sat on a throne of twisted blackthorn branches.

"There are some who say that Bloody Robin is kind to those who come willing," the crone said, stooping, stoking a brazier. "They say he favors the weak, makes them strong in the after. Gives them all the things they never had but wanted." The crone stood, moved to a low wooden table and placed her hand on a gold-hilted knife stuck tip down in the blood black wood.

Balancing on one leg, Hubert lifted the staff high above his head. He'd have one shot only, so he had to make it count. To his horror, he saw his shadow, staff and all, cast on the far wall, betrayed by the light of the brazier.

The crone saw it too, for she wheeled round quick as death, but Hubert was already swinging with all he had.

Crack. A solid, satisfying reverberation travelled through his hands, wrists, arms, all the way to his shoulders. Both Hubert and the crone toppled.

When Hubert looked up, the crone was sprawled backward over the killing table. Eyes closed, yet alive, the rise and fall of her chest barely perceptible, but there nonetheless.

Hubert pushed himself to his feet and glanced around the room. In the far corner he spied a sagebrush broom. Quick as he was able, he hobbled to the broom, then back to the brazier. He pushed the broom inside and held it there until it caught. Then, staff in one hand, burning broom in the other, like some wrath filled wizard rousted from legend, Hubert closed on the wicker.

He knew what he was going to do, held it in his mind certain as a thing already done. He was going to burn the witch's abomination. And when it was burning, he'd torch the cabin, crone and all.

But when he lifted the broom, he caught a gleam in the wicker's black button eyes and a thought occurred unbidden. Hubert imagined himself strong and tall. He imagined his twisted leg straight and sound. Not Hubert the cripple, Hubert the gimp, Hubert the lame. But Hubert the powerful, Hubert for whom the ladies pine.

Almost without thinking, he spoke. "Would you make me handsome? Would you make my jaw strong, my chest broad, my leg straight and true?"

The dead dog's heart thumped in the wicker's chest, but the wicker did not move.

"Would you do these things and more beside?"

Stone still the wicker sat, button eyes dark as endless night.

"Would you do it for a blood sacrifice?"

Slowly, wicker neck creaking, it nodded.

Hubert eyed the crone. A trickle of blood ran from her forehead. The gold-hilted knife caught the light from the burning broom and glinted apple red. Outside, the wind wailed and the bone moon gleamed.

Next! by Preston Dennett [sci-fi]

Just in case you're wondering, you don't dream in cryosleep. At least I didn't. It was black mold that killed me. I never really expected to wake back up. I had just fallen asleep when—what felt like seconds later—I woke up to see several seven-foot-tall cockroaches dressed in white coats surrounding my cryotank.

True to my nature, I began screaming in utter horror. You have to understand, this was my first exposure to seven-foot-tall intelligent cockroaches, and I'm a sensitive guy.

"Do not be afraid, little human," the ugly one said with a distinct cockroachy accent. "We won't hurt you. In fact, we have worked very hard to revive you. We are so glad that you have survived. Please, do not be afraid."

"But I am afraid!" I shouted, and I thrashed around weakly in my tank, unable to get up. "Where am I? Who are you? Where is everyone?"

I was in some sort of hospital room. To my left were all kinds of weird-looking medical equipment. To my right was a large picture window. More tall cockroaches stood there with computer pads and voice-recorders–each of them staring at me.

"If you mean the other humans," said Head Roach, "they're all gone. Humans have been extinct for almost a million years. I'm sorry. You are the only human we know of. It's a miracle we were able to bring you to life."

"Oh, no," I said. "Then it's true? Cockroaches have taken over the Earth. I knew this would happen. We all did. We knew it!"

"Oh, no," said Mr. Bug-Eyes. "You misunderstand. We here," he waved one of his many arms, "we are like you. We have also been revived from cryosleep. Yes, we ruled the Earth for hundreds of thousands of years, after you humans destroyed yourselves. But unfortunately, now our numbers are few. Only a small handful of us still survive."

"Oh," I said, feeling suddenly sorry for Mr. Buggerstein. "Then

Next!

who rules Earth now? Oh God, please don't tell me it's the apes."

"Apes? No."

"Then who?"

"Well..." Bug-Breath seemed to hesitate.

At that moment, the door to the room opened, and in walked an eight-foot, five-hundred-pound bipedal rat, dressed in a soft purple robe.

It waddled forward and put its paw gently in my hand. "Very nice to meet you," it said. "I'm so happy the roaches were able to revive you. An actual human! Our masters will be so proud. They are very excited to meet you."

"Masters?" I squeaked. "You mean, rats don't rule the Earth?"

"No. Oh, we used to. Perhaps it's best we just introduce you."

And in walked one of the new rulers of planet Earth. I recognized it immediately from my shower. Needless to say, I began screaming in horror. Like I said, I'm sensitive.

The roaches all bowed in unison. His Ratness waved his paw with great flourish and said, "May I introduce you to Black Mold."

We've met, I thought, and I continued screaming.

Glass Future by Deborah Walker [sci-fi]

The waitress seems reluctant to come over, pretending not to see us, even though I'd tried to catch her eye several times. We'd ordered our omelets forty minutes ago. How long does it take to crack a few eggs into a hot pan?

"Do you think she's post-human?" I whisper to my husband. She looks too good to be real.

Caleb glances over. "Maybe. She's very pretty, but mods are so subtle, it's difficult to see who's human and who's not."

I wonder why such an attractive looking woman's doing working in a low-rent place like this, a greasy-spoon cafe in a habitat on the edge of Rhea.

We'd booked into the habitat's motel last night. It reeked of overenthusiastic, grandiose plans for the future that would never come true. At dinner, I'd watched motel's guests. I knew them, their small-time liaisons and their wild plans. They didn't want much, just enough to be able to turn up on their home habitat and impress the ones who stayed behind, impress the ones who said they'd never amount to anything. They all ended up here, or someplace like it, scrabbling for success, trying to make a splash in an over-crowded system. This was a place for people who'd never escape the gravity well of their own failures.

It was a sad place to end a marriage.

"Is she ever going to come over?" I ask.

Caleb says, "I see that we *will* get the omelets. They'll be . . . disappointing."

I smile. Caleb has a sense of humor about his gift. Even now, when he knows what I'm about to do, he still keeps cracking jokes.

I take a deep breath and say, "I want a divorce." I wait a moment to see if he's going to make things easier on me. He doesn't say anything. I don't blame him. "I'm so sorry, Caleb."

"So am I." He stares out of the window. "We're on opposite sides of the reflection, Alice. You knew that when you married me."

I look at his reflection in the metal glass window. Caleb was a designer baby. A person designed for space. The multiple copies of his genome in each cell protect him against ionization radiation. But modding is always erratic. There's no way to predict how changes to the genome will affect the body—or the mind. Multiple genome people, like Caleb, developed unusual connections in their brains. Precognition. They remember their future. And all of them are unable to pass the mirror test. They can see their reflections, but they can't recognize themselves. Caleb hasn't got the self-awareness that most human babies develop at eighteen months. That used to fascinate me, that lack of self. It seemed so strange, so exotic—now I find it sad. When love turns to pity, it's time to end the relationship. Caleb didn't deserve my pity.

I look beyond Caleb's reflection to the habitat's garden. Gardens don't thrive in space. The light collected from the solar foils and re-transmitted to the plants is wrong. Earth plants either wither and die or they go wild. The habitat's garden was overgrown and mutated. Swathes of honeysuckle blooms with enormous, monstrous blooms smothered everything. "It's a pretty lousy garden."

"All these mutants should be cut away," says Caleb. "I'm designing Zen gardens for the Oort habitats, swirls of pebbles, low maintenance." A heartbeat later, he says, "Why do you want a divorce, Alice?"

He was going to make me say everything. "I've met somebody else, while you were working on the Oort Cloud project." Caleb's an architect, very much in demand in the ongoing push of colonization.

"Did you?" The note of surprise in his voice is convincing. Caleb's good at pretending to be something other than what he was. Every moment he swims in the seas of his future. Even when he met me, he must have known that one day we'd be here. Poor Caleb. No wonder most precogs end up in hospital, overburdened by the nature of their gifts, or more specifically, overwhelmed by the fact that they're unable to change anything they see. "And you love him?"

"I do. I'm going to move in with him. I'm sorry, Caleb."

"I know."

The waitress comes over. She places two plates of greasy omelets on the table. She looks at Caleb, her violet eyes widening in recognition. Caleb's famous. There aren't too many functioning precogs in the system. Every now and again, someone will put out a documentary about him, usually spurious, about how he's refusing to use his precognition to help people. It doesn't work like that. The future's set. No amount of foreknowledge will change anything.

"Thank you," I say, trying to dismiss her. Just because I don't want him doesn't mean that I want anybody else to have him.

The waitress lingers at a nearby table, straightening the place settings, wondering how she can attract him, thinking that a knowledge of her future might bring her an advantage—just like I did when I met Caleb. She's looking for her future, wanting to use Caleb, not realizing that the only thing we, on this side of the mirror, will ever have are reflections.

"We'll keep in touch, Caleb," I say.

"No, we won't. Goodbye, Alice." He leaves the table, walks over to the waitress. He says something that makes her laugh.

I walk out of the cafe, into the unseen future, without him, stepping into my future, my unseen and unknowable future, without him.

A Mary Shelley Moment by H.L. Fullerton
[horror]

Daddy hasn't been the same since he died. Momma says this is to be expected. "He'll be good as new, Baby Girl. Give him a few days; you'll see." She checks his test results and smiles.

I fear Momma may be batshit crazy. But then I thought dead was dead—no backsies—and Momma's proved that wrong. Least partway. Dead-Daddy can move his eyes, twitch two fingers. Groan some. I see something in his eyes though—a sharpness that makes me move Momma's scalpels, hide all the knives.

This is why Daddy wanted to be cremated, 'cause you can't trust Momma once she gets experimenting. Daddy used to say she's a few theories short of cohesive. But I give her a few days. I miss Daddy, too. Maybe more now that he's back.

Seven days later, Dead-Daddy can get out of bed, almost stand. He makes guttural sounds Momma translates into words. "Waaah."

"You want water? Here's your sippy cup." Momma cries, says how much she loves him.

I'm not convinced the daddy she's brought back is my daddy.

I buy matches, soak rags in gasoline. Momma teaches Daddy to walk, dress himself.

This won't end well. *It can't.*

Momma catches me trying to burn her lab up. She extinguishes the flames and locks me in my room. "I saved you," she says. "Now let me save him."

So I give her time. I wait.

When Daddy's better, I'll show him where I put the scalpels.

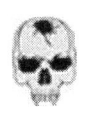

The Mother of Sands by Stewart C. Baker [horror]

Smilšu māte, mother of sands—how I wish I had never heard that name, that I had never learned what waits on the far shore of that river we must cross upon dying. But I have, and I did, and I must share what I witnessed with you, my closest friends.

Last September, I received a letter from the Countess of —, whom I had known as a girl. Although as children we had often played together, I had not heard from her in fifteen years, and was much amazed that she remembered me—let alone that she had thought to send me a letter.

My dearest Clara, the letter began, and went on at some length about the rigors of life amidst the landed gentry which I, in my rented room in gloomy Stepney, cared little to read. Towards the end, though, a section riveted my eyes:

In short, I find myself bereft of the friendship we shared in our youth, and should like nothing more than to renew it. It would grant my fondest hope should you accompany me to my native Riga to visit my mother, who has taken ill.

The letter was signed with my old friend's given name of Ilze. I laughed and shook my head, certain I was the recipient of a passing aristocratic fancy, and nothing more.

A full month passed before I was surprised by a knocking at my door. I opened it, steeling myself to be set upon by some creditor, and met with Ilze's smiling face.

"You did not return my letter," she admonished, "but it does not matter. I have everything prepared."

I sputtered my protests—I had work to do; my creditors would never let me rest—but they fell on deaf ears. Ilze spirited me down the stairs to a waiting carriage, where she plied me with stories of her life. Such was her enthusiasm that I could not so much as speak, let alone request that she return me to my home. Truth be told, I did not try too hard, for while I still felt my old friend would discard me so soon as she grew bored, I had resolved to enjoy the unexpected respite from my worries.

We stopped for the evening in the seaside town of Southend, where Ilze insisted on a shared room at a common inn. I considered it odd that we had not departed by boat from London, and that she had no servants with her; her insistence on sharing a room was doubly strange. But I did not speak of it.

That evening as the sun set, Ilze suddenly paled and rushed me from the inn's dining hall to the room we were to share. I asked what was wrong, but she would say only *Smilšu māte*—the words croaked out from between her lips like a curse and a prayer all at once.

In our quarters, she walked all around with a candle, thrusting it here and there until the shadows danced. At last she placed the candle on the sill, locked the door, and collapsed into bed, sobbing.

I tried to get some sensible response from her, but it was futile. Growing weary myself, I reached for the candle and blew it out, thinking to sleep. But as the light guttered away into night's inky blackness, I saw as clear as day a woman standing over my companion, her eyes pooled shadows in her pinched, drawn face.

My heart hammered in my ears; I scarcely dared breathe, so fearful was I. At length, enough moonlight filtered through the window for me to see the woman was gone. Nonetheless, I could not calm myself, and lay wakeful all through the long night, with only Ilze's hiccoughing sobs for company.

The next morning, we found no sign of the woman, only a small heap of dull, brownish-grey sand. Ilze quaked when she saw this, and quickly scattered it, muttering something in her native tongue, though she would not say why or what.

"It is bad luck to speak of such things," she told me.

"*Smilšu māte?*" I asked. "What does it mean?"

But Ilze only shook her head, and would say no more.

The rest of our trip passed uneventfully. We went by ship to Amsterdam, and from that squat, bustling port travelled again by carriage. Neither in our cabin nor in any of the inns where we stayed did I again see the woman, though on occasion we found small heaps of sand, which Ilze dealt with in the manner of the first.

We arrived in Riga, the heart of old Livonia, on the first of November. You who have never visited that place will know nothing of its cobbled streets. It will mean nothing to you if I speak of the way the stately Daugava flows past the city's many spires, its frigid waters surprisingly strong.

Ilze's mother lived in a narrow three-storey house painted a delicate green. Huddled amidst more expansive buildings, it seemed to cling to the edge of the cobblestones, afraid of losing its place. Ilze clapped at the door and entered without waiting for a response, and I followed her reluctantly, for the building birthed in me a nameless unease.

Inside, the walls pressed in on me. If Ilze felt anything, however, she did not show it. She strode from room to room on the ground floor, calling out in her native language, and did not seem to mind when there was no response.

"Mama must be out," she said with a smile. "Come; I shall show you the sights of the town."

But no sooner had we set out that her face took on its familiar melancholy cast. She became listless, and offered no commentary as we strolled from sight to sight, across age-worn bridges and along the banks of the Daugava. I saw a pleasure steamer plying the waters, festooned with flags and filled with travellers. Marvelling at its existence in this antique place, I mentioned that I should like to try it. But, as ever, Ilze would not be drawn out, and I heard no word from her until we returned to her mother's home, the sun pinking the sky.

A light flickered in the ground floor window, and my earlier unease returned. I found myself looking for sand as Ilze led me inside, and my heart's blood thrummed in my ears as it had that night when I saw the shadow-pooled woman.

Reclining in a chaise lounge was a woman I had never seen before, but who was clearly Ilze's mother: she had the same rich brown hair, the same slightly square face, and the set of her eyes somehow spoke to me, pulling me along despite myself.

"You are late," she said, in slightly accented English. "I had started to fear you would not arrive."

"Oh, mother," Ilze said. "Of course I had to come when I heard you were sick."

"Ha! A year ago and more I sent that letter. A strange form of concern you show me, daughter, when you tarry for so long, and bring an uninvited guest."

Even behind Ilze, I could see her skin flush. "I had pressing business to attend to," she said. "After you sold me to the Count in marriage, my life has not been my own. And it is so remote here that travel alone is—"

"Remote! You speak this way of your native land? I should never have sent you to England, no matter the prize. You—"

Ilze snapped in her native tongue, and her mother responded in kind. Their voices grew louder as they argued, and, not wanting to intrude, I stepped into the next room, where tables were laid out with an astounding feast. Rolls, cheese, and butter by the bowlful; fine cuts of roast and fowl; delicacies I could not name. Balls of dough adorned with hemp seed filled a plate next to pastries overflowing with a thick, white cream.

Where had it all come from, I wondered. I had seen no servants in the house. I popped a pastry into my mouth. Almond paste in the cream, I thought, or something like it—sweet almost to bitterness. Still, I had not eaten in some time. I took another.

At length, the shouting in the next room subsided, and Ilze and her mother entered, their arms entwined for all the world as though they had not just been engaged in a fight of the most intimate sort.

"Your pardon, Clara, dearest," Ilze said. "In this part of the world, we believe it better to air our emotions."

"It is true," her mother said, ushering me into one of the chairs, "no matter what part of the world you find yourself in. You English would be more agreeable did you not bottle up your feelings so. Now sit, and we will show you another of our customs: the feast of the dead."

"All this is for the dead?" The pastries in my stomach heavy as rocks.

Ilze laughed. "Of course not. But it is tradition to give them the first morsel, and the first draught of mead."

"Especially tonight," her mother added, "for on the night after *Simjudas*, the dead can return to wreak justice on those who offend them." And with a light, tinkling laughter, she poured a splash of alcohol into the fireplace, following it with one of the dough balls.

My tongue burned; I only hoped the color did not spread to my cheeks. Neither Ilze nor her mother seemed to notice. Each piled her plate high with food and filled her cup with mead. Reluctantly, I did the same, supposing there was no harm in my inadvertent breaking of their custom so long as they did not know it.

We ate in silence for a time, until, casting around for some topic of conversation, I said to Ilze's mother: "I am glad to see, Mrs. —, that you have regained your health."

The older woman's eyes darkened, and I cursed myself. Why had I brought up the very thing which had caused her and Ilze to erupt earlier?

But after a moment, the older woman smiled and said, "I will tell you how it came about."

And with that she launched into a story that I myself would not believe, were it not for what happened after.

Last year (Ilze's mother said), I caught a coughing sickness. The doctors were unable to cure me, and the prayers of a local priest failed as well. On the 29th of September, I began to cough blood. ("The day is Saint Michael's," Ilze whispered. "The start of the month of the dead.")

Despairing, I walked to the shores of the Daugava. As I crossed one of the river's bridges, a cold wind overtook me and I fell into a coughing fit so violent that my knees went weak. When I recovered, so much blood covered my handkerchief that I resolved to end my life there and then. I leapt into the river, which drew me down into its cold, smothering embrace.

I awoke on a shore I had never before seen: in place of the city were trees of oak and linden, flanked in the distance by rolling hills of a sandy, yellow-grey soil. I was bone wet and shivering, and next to me stood a woman with eyes the color of shadow.

"You have forsaken the traditions," she said to me. "You sent your only daughter to an uncaring land, and your ancestors go hungry."

Her voice was like grit: fine and sharp and hard, impossible to shake free.

"What should I do then, Mother," I asked, shivering from more than damp—for I knew then who she was, and where I had found myself, "to gain your forgiveness?"

"Bring her back," she said. "I will take care of the rest."

With that, she was gone. I staggered to my feet and walked upstream, thinking to return to Riga. When at last I came upon a town, however, it was not my home, but a clump of simple dwellings surrounded by a wall of stakes as thick as trees. The townspeople seemed unable to hear me, and would not meet my eyes...

At that, Ilze's mother stopped talking, lost, it seemed, in reminiscence. Ilze, who had grown progressively paler throughout the recounting, showed no sign of talking.

My own throat dry as parchment, I took a swallow of mead. "What then?"

Ilze's mother looked at me, and her face melted away, replaced by that of the woman I had seen over Ilze's bed that first night of our journey.

"Why then, of course," said the Mother of Sands, "she died." Her voice was just as Ilze's mother had described it.

Before I could react, the candles guttered out and the dark swarmed in with an inhuman shriek. The rest of that night was a blur, all shadow and terror and ash.

In the morning, Ilze and I awoke in our chairs in the banquet room, the tables empty save a patina of dust. Search as we might, the two of us could find no evidence whatsoever that anyone lived in the house. All we found was a heap of yellow-grey sand in the front waiting room, where Ilze's mother had greeted us.

We passed some time huddled together. I was of the opinion that the night's events had been hallucinations brought on, perhaps, by the fatigue of our journey. Ilze, contrarily, believed that we had seen her mother's ghost—that all of it was true, and that *Smilšu māte*, the Mother of Sands, had granted her passage on the night of the feast to visit her absent daughter and take her to that other land by force.

"But you are here with me," I said, "alive."

Ilze only shook her head and sank once more into gloom.

"Come," I said. "I will show us both the truth of life." For I felt a need to be among people.

Ilze allowed me to drag her to the offices of the steamer I had seen the day before. Looking back, I cannot recall what moved me to think that a visit to the river—whence her mother claimed to have died—would take Ilze's mind off the previous night's occurrence. Perhaps it was the steamer itself, the only thing in that city which looked to the future instead of the past. Perhaps some stronger, stranger power was at work.

Whatever the reason, in short order we were aboard the little ship's deck. The steamer was just as I had imagined it: bursting with the energy of a new era, fueled by the powers of men turned to gods. Gliding past the banks of that provincial land suffused me with optimistic health, but all Ilze cared to do was stand and look into the waters of the river. I am afraid I must tell you I left her there, determined that I, at least, would find pleasure in the day's outing.

But we had been out barely half an hour when the boat began to shudder and the deck pitched to one side with a crack and roaring boom. There was another jolt, the air filled with screams, and then the water hit me with a slap of icy cold.

I resigned myself to death, but just before blackness took me, a surge of strength burst through in my limbs; a sudden passion rose in my heart. I would not die here, I resolved—not today! I broke the surface and pushed to the river's edge with surprising ease, shivering in my thin travelling clothes. The river's surface was crowded with boats and men and ropes—a rescue, I thought, but too late, too late for poor Ilze and the rest.

I watched until evening, cold though I was, hoping they would stumble across some survivor—that they would pull my old friend from the water still pink and full of breath.

They found no one. As the rescuers returned to the shore, I asked what had happened, but none answered, lost perhaps in melancholy thoughts of their own. And though I waited by that shore until the moon came full in the sky, I never again saw any sign of Ilze.

Shuddering to think that I had nearly shared her fate, and steadfastly eschewing any thoughts of *Smilšu māte* or Ilze's mother's tale, I left Riga behind me and set off for England.

It was a long, cold journey home, my friends. Without Ilze, I could not afford a carriage or an inn; I dragged myself along the continent's highways, snatching fitful bouts of sleep under trees, in bushes—anywhere I might lie unseen. At first I attempted to beg, but it was as though none could see me. Perhaps it was my lack of any language save English, I thought, or the misery writ in my eyes.

I do not remember what I ate, nor where or how I drank, but I crossed that whole lonely land, and the choppy seas to England. I did these things for you, my dearest friends, for I could not rest until I told you what happened. But now I can delude myself no longer—*Smilšu māte* calls, and I must go.

For I did not survive the steamer's wreck, but drowned in the cold, stately waters of the Dagauva along with the Countess of —, all those many miles from home.

But do not despair.

Though I am leaving you, whom I have just rejoined, we shall meet again. All who live must cross that river's waters, must die and live again on its distant shore. And if ever you see sand in your chambers, or the face of a woman with eyes shadow-shrouded, know that I shall see you soon.

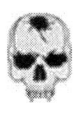

First Date by Doree Weller [horror]

Lauren's palms sweated as she checked her makeup in the mirror. *I hope this date goes well. David is so hot. There's just something about him.* She'd been interested in David for weeks now, but hadn't realized he'd noticed her too until he'd sidled up to her at the company picnic, planted one hand on her ass, and whispered into her ear, "We should go out sometime."

It was sort of an arrogant way to ask for a first date, but at least it was better than the dishonest pick-up lines she normally heard. It seemed like guys rehearsed the lines in front of the mirror and just used them on anything in a skirt. They all had the same fake smile. At least David's ass squeeze was something different. Most guys would've been way too afraid to try something like that at her uber-sexual harassment aware Crap Computer Company, where "We Care About You!"

Lauren didn't fit into the size zero world, and she couldn't figure out what David saw in her, but she felt sexy as she stood in front of the mirror in pantyhose and her best black bra.

David rang the doorbell exactly at seven o'clock, and she grabbed her purse from the table before answering the door. He stood in the doorway, wreathed in shadows. His khaki pants and white button down shirt emphasized his wiry muscles and Lauren's mouth went dry. *I really hope I don't screw this up.*

He held out a bouquet of orange roses. She fumbled with them before taking them. "Oh, thanks. I'm just going to uh, put these in water."

"Can I come in?" he asked.

"Sure. Of course." She opened the door wider and turned away, walking into the kitchen. "Did you, uh…want a drink before we go?"

His voice came from much closer than she expected. "No thanks."

She jolted a little. Taking the flowers out of the cellophane wrapper, she cut the stems under running water and arranged them in a crystal vase. "Thank you. They're beautiful."

"So are you," he replied.

Lauren blushed. *Yeah, right.*

After helping her into the car, he got into the driver's side and pressed a button. Classical music wafted out from the speakers. "That's pretty. What is it?"

"Wagner."

They lapsed into silence, and she fidgeted, pulling down her skirt and wondering if she was exposing too much of her pudgy thighs. The skirt and heels that made her look sexy when she stood up exposed more of her leg than she expected sitting down.

"Relax," he said, and put his hand on her thigh. He gave it a squeeze.

"Why did you ask me out?" she blurted. *Stupid, stupid. You're not supposed to ask questions like that on a first date.*

He laughed, but she didn't think he was laughing at her. "I knew from the first time I met you that you were someone special. I think that you're exactly what I'm looking for."

She was grateful for the darkness as heat rose to her face. "I don't know what you mean."

"You will."

A shiver ran down her spine at his words, and she felt like he was referring to a private joke she didn't quite get. *He's not what you thought he was,* a voice in her head whispered.

"Where are we going?" Lauren asked.

He grinned and glanced over at her. "It's a surprise. I'm hoping you like it."

She shivered again. No dim restaurant and holding hands for this first date. She'd indulged in a fantasy of them sitting side by side in a little booth, heads close, whispering, with him slipping his hand up her skirt to tease her. She was starting to think that nothing she expected would happen today, and wondered if that would be good or bad.

She glanced over at David's profile. *Good. Probably good.* The silence stretched out and grated on Lauren's nerves. Normally she didn't mind the quiet, but she was off balance tonight. *What did people talk about on first dates?* "You, uh, like classical music?" *Well, duh!* She hurried to cover her dumb statement. "What other music do you like?"

David tapped his fingers on the steering wheel. "I mostly stick to classical. I find the music pretty inspirational." He smiled that secret smile again, and Lauren narrowed her eyes. "What music do you like?"

"In general, I just prefer things pretty quiet. Though I could definitely see myself getting used to this." *Did I just sound that desperate? Like, hint, hint, I want to date again. Lame, Lauren. Lame.*

They didn't speak again, and a few minutes later, David pulled off the main road into a wooded area. His car bounced a little as they made their way down the lane to a cabin surrounded by cars. Music and light streamed from the cabin. *There goes my fantasy of a romantic dinner for two.*

They walked up the wooden stairs to the cabin door, and David pushed it open. The pumping bass and screeching guitar got louder. A headache crept in behind Lauren's eyes, but she forced herself to smile.

About ten people milled around. Several people gyrated to the music, red plastic cups in hand. "Let's grab a drink." David took her hand, and the feel of his warm hand in hers was almost enough to make up for the terrible noise that passed for music.

"David!" a man shouted. He put his hand out, as if to shake David's hand, and when David put his hand out, the man slapped his palm and then shook once, firmly. "How you doing, man?"

"Great, Mike. You?"

"Ah, working hard, you know. Who's this pretty lady?" Mike eyed her as if she were something tasty for the grill.

"This is Lauren."

She stuck out her hand, and Mike shook hands with her a little less enthusiastically than he had with David. Mike put a hand on Lauren's back and guided them to the kitchen. "Grab some drinks."

They filled cups with beer from the metal keg on the counter. Lauren sipped, hoping the beer would convince her she was having a good time. Even being with David didn't make the noise less annoying. At least it wasn't crowded.

David and Lauren leaned against the counter, sipping in silence. Several more people came up to David. The men slapped his shoulder or shook his hand, and the women kissed him. Lauren's blood boiled. Maybe the kisses were casual, but she still felt as if the women should be more respectful of his date.

They mingled, talked, and ate hors d'oeuvres. Lauren fought boredom. David kept his hand at the small of her back as he chatted. Several of the other guests tried to draw her into conversation, but her disappointment with the evening didn't let her get very interested. David's secret smile stayed pasted to his lips. It had intrigued her at first, but annoyed her as the night went on.

"How do you know these people?" Lauren asked, knowing she sounded snippier than she wanted to.

"I went to school with Mike about a million years ago. The rest I've met as time goes on."

He turned to get her another beer, and she took a sip. "This tastes funny. Did you put something in it?"

His grin widened. "Maybe."

She fought the urge to throw it at him. "What did you put in here? Why would you put something in my drink?"

He shrugged and looked a bit sheepish. "I just didn't know if it was your first time."

"First time?" She gaped at him. "I've had sex before. You think you need to slip me something so I'll sleep with you?" She shook her head. "We're done here."

"No." He tried not to laugh, but still looked horrified. "No, not sex. Not that I don't want to have sex with you. Of course I do. You're beautiful. But that's not what I meant. I just…"

"I'm not beautiful. Don't screw with me."

His expression turned dark. "Who told you you're not beautiful? I'd like to have five minutes alone with him."

She took a step back as a thrill raced through her.

Something primitive and terrifying flashed in his eyes. He clenched his jaw. "You don't have to be afraid of me. We're soul mates."

Lauren's mouth dropped open. "What? We just met. What are you talking about?"

"I knew from the first time I met you that we were meant to be together. I don't know if you're ready to hear it yet. But I believe it."

"So why the drugs?"

He leaned over and kissed her. She let herself fall into the kiss and wondered if she even cared what he put into the drink.

"The drugs are to make it a little easier for you to accept what's going to happen this evening."

She put the drink aside and met his eyes. "I'll get through it without whatever you put in my drink."

He laughed and gave her a firm kiss on the lips. "You're not supposed to even be able to taste it. I knew I was right about you."

Mike came into the kitchen and Lauren sprang away from David as if they'd just been caught *in flagrante delicto*.

Mike laughed. "Most everyone has cleared out. I think it's time for tequila shots."

David laughed. "I'll slice the lime."

He grabbed two limes from the refrigerator, a plastic cutting board, and a knife from the wooden block.

"I don't like tequila," Lauren said.

David shrugged. "You don't have to drink it. Do beer shots if you want. But come sit with all of us."

Four people were settled around a table in the living room, talking too loud and laughing too much. Lauren's headache pounded like a living thing trying to get out.

Mike poured a shot and pushed it toward Lauren. She shook her head and pushed it back. "Oh, come on. You have to do one."

"No thanks."

"Just one."

David put his hand over Mike's as Mike pushed the shot back toward Lauren again. "She doesn't want one."

Mike looked like he wanted to argue, but then shrugged and he shoved the shot to another woman.

"Is this everyone that's left?" David asked.

"Yeah," Mike replied, doing another shot. "Everyone else is lame and went home early, I guess."

"Well, now the fun can really start."

Mike scowled. "That's right, buddy!"

Leaning over with the knife he used to cut the lime, David sliced the throat of the woman sitting next to him.

For a moment, no one moved. Then at once, the other three people at the table started screaming and shouting. Mike moved toward David, and David plunged the knife into the bigger man's stomach. A woman tripped as she tried to run away.

Lauren watched, as if from a distance. Numbness cloaked her, and she wondered if it were the drugs. Then she remembered that she hadn't had any drugs. David had wanted her to have some because he didn't know if it was her "first time." *Is this what he meant?*

The second man tried to help the fallen woman up, and David ducked low and sliced. The man screamed and clutched his ankle. The woman on the ground covered her face and sobbed.

"Lauren. Hey, Lauren."

She looked up and met David's eyes. The secret smile was still on his face, and his eyes gleamed. "There's some duct tape in the drawer in the kitchen. Be a sweetheart and grab it for me, would you?"

Lauren stood up automatically and wandered into the kitchen. She looked through the drawers and realized that she wasn't seeing anything in them. Taking several deep breaths, she forced herself to slow down and made another search, finding the duct tape quickly this time. On her way out, she grabbed a knife from the wooden block.

Hurrying back into the living room, she found the scene the same as when she'd left it. The woman continued to cower at David's feet, and the man still clutched his ankle, sobbing. He was also bleeding from several stomach wounds, and Lauren guessed he'd probably tried to get away. Despite the blood on his white shirt, David still looked handsome.

She held the duct tape out to him.

He glanced at the knife, then back at her. "What are you going to do with that thing?"

She followed his eyes to the knife clutched in her hand and shrugged, feeling suddenly shy.

"Come here," he ordered, beckoning with the knife.

Heart racing, she walked toward him. He pulled her in for a kiss. Her toes curled by the time he broke the kiss. "I know what you want," he whispered.

Taking the tape from her hand, he leaned over the sobbing woman and grabbed her bicep. "Come on, get up." His voice sounded gentle, and after more urging, the woman responded and stood at his direction. He taped her hands behind her back and taped her to the chair. David looked up at Lauren. "Do you want her gagged?"

Lauren shook her head quickly, eyes wide.

After he secured the woman, he taped the man's hands and feet together. The man fought, but blood loss made him sluggish.

David went to the stereo and flipped off the music. "You prefer no music, right?" Without waiting for an answer, he went back out to the kitchen and grabbed two glasses and a bottle of wine. Lauren stood in the middle of the room, gripping the knife, not really sure what to do.

"Please. Please!" the woman sobbed.

Lauren looked at her, eyes wide.

David came back in and sat on the couch. He patted the seat beside him and poured two glasses of wine. He put the wine bottle on the coffee table and leaned back. After a brief hesitation, Lauren walked over and sat down. She looked at the knife, then put it on the coffee table and sat back with her own glass of wine.

David stretched his arm over her shoulders. "So, tell the truth. Have you ever killed anyone before?"

Lauren shook her head. "Not a person."

"What, then?"

Lauren shrugged and tried to sound casual. "Stray cats, dogs, that kind of thing."

David sounded far away as he reminisced. "Yeah, I started that way too, but I killed my first woman during sex. She liked it rough, and

I ended up choking her. Once you have your first kill, you can't go back." He squeezed her shoulder. "I'd be much more careful with you, Lauren. I've never met a woman like you. I knew from the first moment I met you. I saw it in those beautiful eyes."

"I always thought there was something wrong with me," she whispered.

He shook his head and turned her so she faced him. "There's nothing wrong with you. Not a single thing."

"I'm so glad you found me," she said. Feeling bolder, she straddled his lap and kissed him deeply with the sound of the woman's pleas in the background. When she broke the kiss, she snuggled against his chest as he stroked her hair with a feather light touch.

"Oh God, please don't do this. Please let me go. I won't tell anyone, I swear. Please."

Lauren looked up at David and frowned. "She's really starting to get on my nerves."

He nodded. "Yeah, I usually gag them and put on some classical music. We can try it that way next time."

"Okay."

"Give me one second to get something out of my car." He went outside, and for a second, Lauren thought he was going to leave without her. Instead, he brought in a small paper bag and fished white rose petals out, spreading them around. "I thought these would look nice with all the red."

The woman had started to sound hoarse.

"Ready for your first?"

Lauren smiled and slid off the couch. She grabbed the knife and walked over to the woman. David sat on the couch, sipping his wine and smiling. Lauren used the knife to make little cuts in the woman's arm, her chest, her cheek. After several minutes of her screaming and whimpering, Lauren grabbed the duct tape and slapped it over the woman's mouth. *Much better.* She continued making tiny cuts, enjoying the blood flowing. After a long time, the woman stopped responding, and Lauren got ready to plunge the knife into her stomach.

"Wait!" David ordered, pulling himself off the couch. He grabbed his knife and hurried over.

Lauren frowned.

David smiled sheepishly. "I thought we could do the first one together." He aimed his knife at the man's belly and looked at her.

She smiled and blew him a kiss.

"On three then. One... two... three..."

Their eyes still locked, they plunged their knives in at the same moment, and Lauren felt pleasure wash over her. She shivered.

David was at her side in an instant, gripping her arms. "Cold?"

"No. I don't think I'll ever be cold again. Not with you here."

They sat back on the couch, sipping wine and enjoying watching the woman and man bleed out. Stomach wounds were a painful death, and watching it was better than TV. When they finished the wine, David said, "It's time to clean up now."

Lauren looked around. "Our fingerprints are everywhere."

"I'm usually more careful, but this first time, I wanted it to be decadent for you. So, we're going to burn it down. I have gas and spare clothes in the car for both of us, and we're going to shower here and burn it all."

"You're so thoughtful."

"I wanted it to be just perfect. Was it okay for you?"

Lauren felt warmed by the uncertainty in his voice. She stood on tiptoes and brushed a kiss over his lips. "It was just perfect," she whispered against them.

When Lauren went into the bathroom to shower, she glanced in the mirror and marveled at the change in her appearance. She was beautiful. And she had her own secret smile now. She was finally free.

Her lips curved and her eyes sparkled.

David would never look at another woman.

Never.

She would make sure of it.

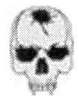

Dragon Dance by H.A. Titus [fantasy]

"Want to come with me tonight?" my brother asked, poking his head in at my door.

He never invited me on his midnight rambles. Before, I would have jumped at the chance. Now...I turned and stared through the crack in my curtains. White powder like gypsum dust covered everything, sparkling under the starlight. A shiver spidered up my back.

I pulled my blanket up around my shoulders.

The floor creaked. My brother sat down on the edge of my bed, pulled his bare feet up to the mattress and wrapped his arms around his knees.

"It's not the end of the world."

"It may as well be," I muttered. The clock on my desk rattled as it rolled over to a new hour. I glanced at it. Only three a.m. "Why did you bother me?"

He shrugged. "You were awake."

Of course I was awake. The nights seemed never-ending now, and the days I spent listlessly doing school and chores and gulping caffeine, hating every moment I had to step outside. The cold worked its way into my bones and made me feel like I'd never be warm again, even when I was curled in my thick comforter. Icicles had frozen in my insides.

I missed the warm sun and sandy beaches.

He pulled on my arm. "Come on."

I glared at him. How had he adjusted so quickly to the north? "No."

His face tightened. "If you could just see what I've found..."

"What?" I bit my tongue. Why had I spoken?

"You'll have to see."

"That's cheating." I sighed. Well, this little mystery would at least pass an hour. I slid out of bed, and my toes curled from the wooden floor. I pulled my socks higher, slid into my slippers, and pulled on my fuzzy robe. We crept downstairs, and my brother stopped at the back door, grabbing his boots and parka.

I recoiled. "We're not going outside?"

"You have to see it."

A harsh *no* stood on the tip of my tongue, ready to launch at him. His eyes twinkled, and he grinned. The sight made me pause. Mister No-Emotions, excited? I had to see whatever this was now.

I jerked my parka down from its hook. "You're going to regret this."

He shook his head and pushed open the door.

The night air tasted cold. I drew a deep breath into my tingling lungs and stared into the sky. The sky was such a smooth, beautiful black, studded with flecks of diamonds unsullied by city lights. However beautiful it was, the chill made my jaw tighten.

My eyes caught a flicker near the horizon. Above the hills, ribbons of blue, green, and red danced to a tune I thought I could hear in the falling snow—sharp, like needles against glass, but sweet. My muscles relaxed just a little as I strained to follow the melody.

My brother's warm hand slipped into mine and his words interrupted the snowflakes' song. "C'mon, it gets better."

We jumped off the deck and sank to our knees in a snowdrift. I wanted to stop and try to find the song of the snowflakes again, but he pulled me onward. We crunched through the snow, our boots drowning out any other sound.

Near the top of the first hill, he tugged me down to my knees. "Be quiet from here, or else they'll see you."

"Who?"

"Ssh."

He crept up the hill. I followed, trying to keep my parka from rustling too much. When we got to the top of the hill, my brother pointed down into the valley.

I covered my hand with my mouth to contain a gasp.

I would have barely been able to see the creatures below, save for the colors. Brilliant emerald green, deep crimson, midnight blue sparked off the dancing limbs and shot up to join the ribbons moving in the sky.

I'd always thought dragons to be ungainly, but as they danced, their tails and wings fluttered out to keep them in perfect balance. They twined into long blurs of colors—blue interwoven with green, green kissing crimson, crimson stroking blue again. Their heads bobbed and tucked, their long necks graceful in the moonlight.

They sang as they danced. Their song was wordless and deep, vibrating the snow underneath us. The notes shivered through me, joined with the needles-against-glass song of the snowflakes. The song blended together, earth-wrenching bass and heavenly soprano, a harmony and a melody in white in the steam from creatures' mouths and the delicate crystals of the snowflakes. The lights in the sky, ever increasing, mimicked the movements of the dance. Their paws skimmed the snow, packed and melted from the touch of their warm scales.

The dragon scales may as well have been touching me. My body was still cold, but the tightness eased away. The icicles that had been growing inside me for the past few months melted, and I could actually feel my heart pumping blood again. Why had I moped inside for so long?

With a final whirl, the dragons furled their wings about their bodies. The light vanished. The ribbons in the sky faded out. The valley dimmed into gray, dingy snow. The stars appeared in the sky, but they seemed flat and dull after the dance.

I turned to my brother. "What was that?" The words were thick in my mouth, clumsy after the grace of the dragons.

My brother's eyes sparkled with something other-worldly. "That was the dragon dance."

"Dragon dance." Beautiful.

My brother stood and headed down the hill. As I followed, I looked up at the sky. Snowflakes stung my eyes, stuck to my eyelashes. If only there was one more ribbon of light left…

But the sky was black velvet again.

Strangely enough, the thought didn't make me sag as it should have. As I reached the bottom of the hill and took my brother's hand, I glanced over my shoulder. Just a quick glance to say goodbye. To say thank you for the contentment coursing through my body.

For a moment, a section of snow blurred.

For a moment, the snowflakes drifting into my hair turned emerald green.

For a moment, I thought I saw a dark green eye, winking at me through the swirling snow.

In that moment, I knew I was invited back. Welcome even. The dragons had enjoyed my presence at their dance.

Copy That by Holly Schofield [sci-fi]

"More salt, would ya," Colin instructed the restaurant's 3D food fabber, then chucked his French fries in its tableside hopper. It whirred, then lit up with a thank you.

"There's a salt shaker right on the table." Miranda pursed her lips.

"Huh?"

"You could have added salt yourself." She waved her hand at the tiny plastic shaker before picking up her BLT sandwich.

"I thought that was, you know, just decorative," Colin said, watching his fries reassemble themselves layer by layer through the small, greasy viewing window of the fabber. "Besides, that wouldn't get salt all the way through each fry. Like, inside of them?" *Stupid fabber.* It should have got it right the first time.

Suddenly he wished he'd splurged for somewhere fancier than this Print & Go diner, like the Alto Heaven Eatery down the street. They had real human waiters who scraped your plate off for you if you needed your dinner refabbed. If they'd eaten there, Miranda might be giving him one of those crooked smiles of hers right now instead of just watching the restaurant window gradually opaque as the setting sun struck it.

This was their third date and so far she'd only smiled a little. He wanted so badly to make her laugh.

The fabber beeped and he retrieved his plate of fries from the delivery tray before it fully extended.

"How was work today?" Miranda raised her cute little eyebrows as she bit through the blurred P&G logo on her sandwich into the precise and even layers of brown, green, and red. She had asked this question on their other two dates and he was never sure why.

"Some guy wanted original wiper blades for his '14 Chevy-Dai." Colin chuckled at the memory, juggling a fry between his hands. "Ouch, now they're too hot. Prickin' restaurant." He contemplated running his plate through the fabber again at a cooler setting, but settled for blowing on each one instead. "I said he should wait a month until the windshields with the new 4D responsive coating are available. Who needs wipers when the windshield turns water-repellent in the rain?" A wink seemed too much, so he delivered the punch line deadpan: "I told him he should take his old wiper blades and stash them with his buggy whip."

"Huh? Oh, you mean, they're outmoded now. I get it." Miranda's smile was brief. She put down her sandwich. "Colin, have you ever thought of trying for a different job, one that isn't just—oh, never mind." She laid a hand on his, and his heart thudded.

"Isn't just what?" He could have sat there for hours, just enjoying the touch of her fingers.

"Never mind, sweetie. Change of topic—I went to see Grandma today." Miranda bit her lip. "I need to talk about it, I think."

Her grandfather's death two weeks ago had hit her hard, especially since the old guy had died of liver failure just days before Federal template approval for internal organs had come through. Miranda hadn't laughed since. Colin swallowed and groped for the right words. "Has your Grandma settled in at the retirement home?"

Miranda nodded, picked up her sandwich again, but didn't take a bite. "She finally unpacked her stuff, including a ton of photo albums. She showed me a picture of Grandpa in a suit and tie for one of their Saturday night dates. He used to give her wild daisies wrapped up in a sheet of newspaper. Isn't that the sweetest thing?"

"Yeah, copy that. Your Gramps had style. And your Grandma could keep the newspaper to remember the day's events by." That was one of the functions of newspapers back then, Colin was pretty sure.

Miranda beamed and ordered a coffee refill—apparently, he was on a roll.

"Too bad your Grandpa didn't have gene-modded flowers back then, all those crazy colors and shapes. And, hey, a home printer—he could have made customized wrapping paper. They had 2D printers back in the '60's, didn't they?"

Miranda's face fell. *Wrong thing to say. Crap.* He reached out a hand towards her, but she drew back.

"You just don't get it, do you? Not everything has to be fresh-printed." She poked a finger at his head. "Is there a real you inside there or is *that* fabbed?" She grabbed up her purse. The *beep* as the screen presented the bill to Colin was drowned out by the restaurant door closing behind her.

The hairdresser's door chimed as Colin entered. Acrid chemicals hurt his throat. The mirrored room seemed larger than it was, ping-ponging the reflections of the five stations into infinity. The five customers, their hair wet and messy, looked up from their chairs. Two skinny male hairdressers glanced over, then resumed their work. Miranda, in a pale blue form-fitting tunic, stood by the farthest chair, brushing something purplish onto the hair of a large woman.

Colin, using the courage he'd found after three sleepless nights, walked the gauntlet towards her, keeping one hand behind his back.

"Can you take a break?" The eyes of the watching women tickled the back of his neck and he fiddled with today's earring, an exact miniature of his favorite reality star in last night's costume.

"No, Colin, I can't. Whatever you have to say, say it here."

"Here? Uh, okay, if you don't mind your customers overhearing. Don't want to lower your, uh, prestige."

"Prestige? Colin, you think I'm a hairdresser because of *prestige?*" Miranda shook her head, still plastering the vile-smelling goo on the woman's head.

"You've got a great job, one that requires a person to do it. Like me with my automotive supply advisor position." He brushed his knuckles across the Vehicle Hands logo on his uniform shirt.

"I'm not in it for the prestige, Colin. I'm in it for the people I meet. Copy *that?*"

He'd put his foot in it once again. *Damn.* But he'd come this far; he might as well finish it.

"Here. For you." He drew out the flowers. The fat lady craned her neck up and clapped her hands, her long nails—fabbed like dragon talons—clacking together. Behind him, several women chuckled and said things he didn't listen to. Miranda froze and the paint from her brush dripped on the floor.

He thrust the paper cone at her. "I got the newspaper in an antique store," he said, the words spilling out of him. "Nineteen sixty-seven, that's when your grandparents were first dating, right? And it's a summer date, June 23rd, that's about when daisies bloom, isn't it?" He paused to draw in a breath. The yellowing scrap of newspaper had cost him a week's pay when he could have fabbed it for pennies, but that didn't matter. The light in Miranda's eyes—that mattered.

"Those aren't daisies," the fat woman said, violet rivulets running down her neck, staining the white towel.

He kept his eyes on Miranda. "Yeah, these ones are all yellow. I couldn't find any daisies anywhere. No template or anything." He sounded stupid, to his own ears, but the women all nodded and murmured among themselves.

"Even the crab grass is disappearing," one woman said, "now that sidewalk slabs are fabbed to fit so tightly."

"Then I thought of the zoo. The animals have those open fields they roam on, so I climbed a stone wall into the Africa zone—"

"You went into a lion cage for me?" Miranda interrupted him. Her mouth was all screwed up. *What did that mean?*

"You picked dandelions!" exclaimed the grey-haired lady one chair over, her curlers bobbing in her enthusiasm. "I haven't seen one in years!"

"Yeah, sure, that's what they are." He laid the limp bundle on Miranda's hairdressing stand. The whole thing seemed silly now.

"Colin! Like Grandpa used to do?" Miranda's eyes filled with tears.

"I'm sorry. I didn't mean—" Colin broke off when Miranda stepped closer and took his hand.

Her mouth twisted into a smile. "Dandelions! From the lions!" Her laughter, when it came, was rich and sweet and seemed to bounce endlessly back and forth between the mirrors that surrounded them.

The Silver Witch by Tara Calaby [fantasy]

When the townspeople found Rosalind sitting astride the mayor's daughter with her skirts hoisted to her thighs and her bodice loosened at the chest, they knew she was a witch. She was feasting at her victim's lips, sucking the soul out of poor Leda's body as she lay, bent, in the shadow of the mill. The preacher was summoned and, although Leda protested, Rosalind was shackled and presented to the mayor for trial.

On the first day, three witnesses were called. The miller stood with flour on his shirt and stammered as he told the townspeople that Rosalind had been seen near his mill before. Once, he had watched her gathering flowers and, the next day, the crooked form of a bird's embryo had been found in the nearby grass. "And she never took a husband," he finished. Indeed, she had turned the miller down.

The preacher quoted from his prayer-book and tugged at his clothing when he spoke. It had been months, he revealed, since Rosalind had last breached the chapel's doors. "Witches," he told them, "are not able to step on holy ground." The people gasped, but Rosalind stood, silent, and faced the preacher with a frozen jaw.

Leda's chastity and piety were lauded by the goldsmith's son, whom she had been betrothed to at the age of thirteen. Her fear of God could be seen in her unwillingness to be alone with him, for she obviously feared that the devil might tempt her to go astray. "She is innocent to the sins of the flesh," he vowed. "It is no wonder that a witch should covet the whiteness of her soul."

On the second day, Leda petitioned her father on bended knees. She clasped the hem of his woven coat and wept tears that streaked her pale cheeks with silver in the weak winter's light. He patted her head and praised her mercy and forgiveness. "You are a good woman," he said, "and will make an obedient and faithful wife. The witch will be punished for preying upon one so untouched by the hands of evil."

In desperation, Leda stood, and clutched the mayor's folded

hands. "She did not prey upon me! I submitted willingly to her embrace."

The people gasped and flushed with fear, and the preacher muttered prayers into the collar of his shirt. Rosalind stayed silent but, when her eyes met Leda's, she shook her head. The mayor flinched, but stood to speak his part. "The witch speaks through my daughter's tongue! She must die, so that Leda may be freed!"

As Rosalind was led away, Leda fell to the ground and drew patterns in the dust at the mayor's feet.

The wood was damp, and the kindling sparked and sputtered in a light fall of snow. The townspeople clustered around the pyre, with the preacher in their midst. Leda was held upright at the mayor's side, and Rosalind's wrists were bound to the wood behind her back. Her eyes stung from the smoke and floating embers, but she did not weep as the slow flames warmed the soles of her boots.

The people fell silent as the fire rose. Leda closed her eyes against the sight and whispered words of desperation as she rested her cheek against her father's broad chest. Rosalind stood, eyes fixed, and waited to burn.

At first, it appeared to be a trick of the setting sun. Where once it had been colored by the crimson and gold of the flames, Rosalind's body began to glow with a silvery light. As the fire caught the thin fabric of her skirts and climbed towards her waist, she did not scream, nor even whimper, but instead remained stoic while the cloth turned to ash and the flames pressed against her naked skin. The mill cast its tall shadow over the marketplace and, in the greying light, pink flesh took on gleaming silver lines.

The preacher's voice rose in condemnation. "Only the devil," he said, "could wield such fiendish power." Within the flames, Rosalind laughed, and her breath was a spark of molten silver. She did not die. The silver was tempered by the fire, becoming ever brighter, and her form became fluid and blinding in the heat.

The mayor ordered water to be brought from the well, and the goldsmith's son threw bucketful after bucketful, and eventually quenched the pyre's flames. Rosalind stood in the circle of charred, sodden wood, and shone with icy heat as the jailer reached to bind her hands. As he touched her, he shouted, and his palms were blistering even as he washed the molten metal from his skin. The miller poured water over her head, but it turned to steam and rose, harmless, into the air.

When Rosalind walked through the ashes and away from the town, no one stood in her way.

In the meadow beside the mill, Leda awaited Rosalind with her hands twisted in a knot of concern. Rosalind threaded now-cool fingers through Leda's hair, and pressed smooth silver lips against Leda's warm cheek.

"I'm sorry," Leda said, tracing the lines of Rosalind's face with her fingers. "It was the only magic I knew that might keep you alive."

Rosalind stilled Leda's words with the palm of her hand. She wrapped icy arms around Leda's waist and warmed plated lips with the heat of Leda's mouth. The moon pushed the clouds aside and the young witch shone silver in Rosalind's reflecting light.

Born to It by Tara Calaby [fantasy]

It is said among our people that a third daughter of a third daughter will possess the power of the devil's sight. Anne was pointed of face and timid of character, unlike her older sisters Mary and Katerina, who delighted their schoolmates so much with their fair looks and easy humor that it was easy to forget their humble status. There were other siblings—two boys and a girl, if I remember correctly—but they did not take classes with us, as even the oldest was not long weaned. Their mother was a pale and inconsequential creature, who wafted about our town as though she were not entirely connected to the world she inhabited.

Anne was the plain child of the family, an affliction that was not made any easier by the peculiarity of her nature. She was certainly talented at her lessons, often coming fourth or even third in our year, but in conversation her words were stilted, almost as though she had little knowledge of her mother tongue. We were wary of her long before we had cause to be. It may have been something in her eyes, or possibly just the dated cut of her well-patched dress.

Without the benevolence of Mr. Wrottesley, Anne would not have entered our world at all. It was a fact that his daughter, Isadora, was well aware of. As our schoolgirl leader, Isadora guided our opinions, and her resentment of what she considered her father's lavish spending of her inheritance on the unworthy offspring of his mine workers had ensured Anne's unpopularity long before her actions led us to fear her.

In fact, she spent five terms under Miss Patridge's care before her true nature was exposed. On Thursdays, the wealthier members of our class took riding lessons. For those of us whose fathers were not capable of maintaining the cost of feeding and stalling a horse used only for frivolous pursuits, it was a cause of great envy. Although my father was only a merchant, I was favored by Isadora for my quick brain, and I remember well the occasions when she would call me from the circle of watching girls and allow me to ride her chestnut mare for a few wonderful minutes. Anne, however, was not so blessed. She was a favorite of no one, and usually sat alone while we watched the horses and riders go through their paces.

On the day in question, however, she paced at the edge of our group, wringing her hands and pulling fingers through her dark hair until it was wild and loose around her face. Finally, Elsa—who was always as quick-tempered as she was inquisitive—stilled her with a hand that clutched a little too tightly, confirmed by the crimson mark it left on Anne's pale arm.

"Did you sit upon an ants' nest?"

A few of the other girls laughed, but Anne's eyes remained dull, almost as though she had been blinded. "She is lost," was her only reply. "She is lost, lost, lost."

I shivered at her words, but Elsa was not so moved. "Who is lost, you peculiar girl? We're all here; can't you see?"

"Lost," Anne repeated in that strange, dark voice. "Constance is lost." She gasped, as though choking on her own breath, and reached a hand towards the riding ring before crumpling to the ground.

So eerie did she look, and so grey and lifeless, that we clustered around her with little thought to our usual aversion. Emily patted Anne's hand, Elsa shook her roughly, and even I pressed my palm to her clammy forehead, as though it might somehow help. Such was our surprise and confusion that we barely noticed a shriek from one of the riders, dismissing the ensuing clamor of voices as mere reaction to Anne's collapse. She lay there as though dead, her chest barely rising with each breath. Her stillness frightened me and I couldn't help but rise and break through the crowd of my schoolmates in order to fan my face and drink deeply of the autumn air.

In the ring, the horses shuffled nervously, abandoned by their riders. Isadora was bent over a dusty form, the other girls linked in an arc around them. Lydia's face was buried in the lace of Clara's dress, while Clara herself pressed a handkerchief to her mouth.

"She's dead," Isadora announced, and I felt a hand upon my waist as Emily moved to my side.

There was silence, save for the bird calls, until a soft moan from Anne shattered our stupor. We turned and, as Anne opened her eyes, Emily pointed to her and spoke, her voice shaking but defiant.

"Witch."

It is in our nature to be afraid of the things that we do not understand. Perhaps it is also our greatest failing. We are superstitious as a people, reared upon whispered tales of the devil while we are bounced upon our mother's knees. We are born to fear, and often governed by it.

I, too, fell under its spell.

After the funeral, Anne became more of a shadow than ever before. Where she previously had been merely avoided, she now became actively ostracized. The bolder girls called her names to her face, while the rest of us gossiped about her in tones that were not quite hushed enough to escape her notice. Her lack of reaction encouraged, rather than dissuaded, us. It seemed akin to an admission that she was everything we accused her of being.

Under the bombardment of our words, Anne grew smaller and sharper. The greys of her darkened and transformed, giving her skin a sickly, even greenish, hue. Her dark hair, always disheveled, was loosed from the customary pins and ribbons, and she began to wear it hung in snake-like waves about her face. We shrank from her gaze, in terror of what those sunken eyes might see.

All was calm, however, for a time. The leaves browned, then fell, and snow enfolded the schoolhouse in its icy embrace. Spring was late that year, but when the warmth came, the trees sprouted their greenery with rare vigor. In the sunlight, our fears were muted, yet our hatred had become a habit that clung to our skin. And always we waited, waited for it to happen again.

The hill that divided our town from the next was circled by a slate-covered path. Miss Patridge often led us on rambles to the peak, hunting rare wild-flowers for our presses and drawing our attention to the birds that nested in the overhanging trees. Isadora, despite her frail appearance, was a strong athlete, and she usually led our ragged line.

The sun was hot on our faces that afternoon, as we wove past slate outcrops and dodged the twisting roots that veined the path. Clara's light soprano accompanied our footsteps, and laughter echoed from the stone face of the cliffs above. I remember Isadora's face as she turned to call back to a friend—the way the light caught the angles of her face and lit her golden hair. And then there was a scream, and a rush of footsteps, and I was pushed roughly to the ground.

"No!" Anne shouted, twisting a hand in the folds of Isadora's skirt.

I picked slate and dirt from my bleeding palms, while Isadora regarded Anne with scornful eyes. "This dress is worth more than your father earns in a year. I advise you not to tear it."

"No further." Anne clung tighter still, restraining Isadora when she attempted to pull away. "Please."

As Isadora bent to physically loosen Anne's grasp, there was a loud crack from above, as though a storm was splitting the cloudless sky. We looked towards the heavens, but it was from the rock face ahead of us that the rain appeared, a brief shower of stone followed by the dull thunderclap of a boulder striking the ground.

Isadora stood straight-shouldered above the folded body of Anne, whose gasping breaths punctuated the silence while dust filled the air. Slowly, Lydia walked towards them, ignoring Anne as she wrapped arms around Isadora's waist. I remember the cry of a willowbird and dull pain in my hands and knees. The whispers ceased. Anne rose and we looked away.

Although Isadora's survival marked the end of our open accusations and mockery, Anne was not to linger long in Miss Patridge's class. A flood in the mine carried off her father, along with six other boys and men. The town was appropriate in its sympathies, sending food and flowers to the grieving families, but such gestures do not last long and Anne's mother was fit little for parenthood and not at all for employment. Mary and Katerina remained in school, protected by the likelihood that they would more easily find worthy husbands if they had the letters and sums to manage a house. Anne, however, would not marry. Even if there had been a boy left in the town who was not wary of her powers, no priest would have allowed her in his church. And so it was that she was seen gathering her meagre possessions into a worn bag one Sunday afternoon, destined for a new life earning food for her family in whatever manner she might find.

Isadora and I were painting landscapes in the garden when Anne closed the school gate for the final time. We had never spoken of that day, at Isadora's request, but Anne's quiet departure loosened my tongue.

"Will you do anything for her?"

She added a light streak of vermilion to the sky on her canvas, then stood back to survey her work before replying. "A witch has the devil's assistance."

"But if she is not?"

"She is not my responsibility."

The paint—too thin—ran, streaking her painting with dripping blood. Isadora wrenched the canvas from her easel and tossed it to the ground as she walked away.

Months passed before I saw Anne again.

In late summer, Isadora invited me to her family's grand house on the edge of our town. We ate strawberries in the garden, dipping them in cream that tasted of lavender and rose. She showed me their private stream, and the way that the fish that lived within it would rise to the surface to be tickled by a gentle touch. I watched as her dogs flushed blackbirds from the trees and we laughed together as though girls of only six or seven springs.

When the shadows stretched across the grass, we retired inside. In the parlor, Isadora rang a silver bell and we were brought tea sweeter and more complex of flavor than any my father had ever sold. At first, I did not notice the maid who stood, with dark head bowed, waiting for us to finish. It was only when her hand brushed against mine as she bent to tidy the china that I registered her presence. Her skin was cold and yet somehow felt feverish at the same time. I gasped and our eyes met. I knew her.

Isadora spoke as soon as we were alone, anticipating the question that I had dared not ask. "There's a shortage of properly trained servants these days," she said, her eyes fixed on the wall behind me. "My previous maid was called away and, for wont of anyone with the appropriate background, I suggested to my father that Anne might do."

My thoughts were a tangle but I remembered my place. "And does she?"

"You would think that she'd been born to it."

As Isadora walked me to the door, I felt Anne's gaze follow us from the gloom beneath the stairs. I cannot say whether it was a witch who watched us, or just a lonely girl, but I was glad to feel the last warmth of the setting sun upon my face as I climbed into the Wrottesleys' carriage. I had looked into Anne's eyes and seen a darkness there that I could not explain—and cannot, even now, forget.

Transition by Fred Waiss [fantasy]

"The Johnson boy came out today."

"Yeah? What did he choose to do?"

"Fly, of course. Just like his parents."

"Kid never did have any imagination."

"Oh, I don't know. I think it must be nice for the whole family to fly together. To just step out the front door and sail into the air and go anywhere you like. It's what the majority of people choose, you know. It always has been."

"Oh boy do I know! People filling up the skies with no controls, no traffic rules, no safety requirements. Flying collisions have replaced accidental overdoses as the leading cause of death.

"The Job Authority has tried to figure out something, but no one knows what they can do. Traffic lights and traffic lanes in the air? In three dimensions? And even if they could, it wouldn't cut out the accidents from joy-flying over the lake."

"Oh, no. Is that what you did again today?"

"Three kids stunting and goofing off over the lake last night. That nonsense is dangerous enough during the day. But in the dark? And with alcohol? There's a thin line between reckless and stupid. The kid reported his two friends crashed into each other and went down. They didn't come up."

"Did you find them, Dad?" Their daughter, Margie, had been listening while reading her homework.

He looked at her solemnly and nodded. "It took a while. He couldn't tell us where they went down since it happened at night and he wasn't paying much attention. Aquaman would ask the fish and find out. Instead, I just swam around in ever-widening circles until I found them."

"Dad, no offense, but you don't look much like Aquaman anyway."

He looked at himself, shrugged, and grinned a little. "Yeah, I know." He ran his hand over his thin dark hair and the inevitable facial stubble of early evening. He patted the large area just above his belt. "I'm afraid my family tends to carry around more weight than we need. Sorry I passed that on to you, Kiddo."

His wife chipped in, "Don't take all the blame, John." Marsha, blonde and still pretty, carried more pounds than necessary, just like her husband. "Unfortunately, I contributed my share of 'weighty' genes too."

Margie returned to the previous subject. "That sounds pretty tedious, just swimming around in circles."

"But I still enjoy the water. I wouldn't have minded at all except that the lake is so muddy. That made it hard to see and hard to breathe. Like walking through a dust storm. After I'd carried the bodies ashore I had to stick my head in the cleaning tank for fifteen minutes just to wash my lungs out and get all the guck out of my eyes."

"Dad, why do you do it? Didn't the JA give you any other options?"

"Sure. I could have been an underwater demolitions guy, but I wouldn't be home much and rigging or defusing bombs did not appeal to me, especially after I met your mother."

He turned to his wife. "And how was your day, Honey?"

She shrugged. "About average. Two idiots tried to smuggle bags of drugs in their intestines. The x-ray machine won't catch that, but I do. And one aspiring hijacker tried to get through with a plastic gun in his crotch. But these eyes are better than any x-ray machine.

"At least I get a change of pace. Tomorrow's my rotation day at the hospital."

"Mom, isn't that gross? Seeing people's insides, seeing broken bones and tumors, and digestion, and all that nasty stuff?"

"It was at first. But I've been seeing it since I turned 15. I'm used to it by now. And in both jobs, I get to save lives, so it's more than worth it. Besides, that's what I chose.

"And on the subject of 15, you're coming up on that, Margie. Have you decided yet what you're going to do?"

"No. But I have decided sort of what I want. I want something that will be fun. And I don't want something that the stupid Job Authority can make un-fun!"

"Tall order, Kiddo." remarked her father. "Not the fun part. Whatever you choose can be fun...for about three years. When you turn 18, the JA will have decided how to turn you into a productive member of society.

"Used to be, one of the favorites, especially of small boys, was to be really strong. Lift-500-pounds-strong. That became less popular when they realized the JA would assign them to loading trucks and ships and trains, or moving furniture.

"How did school go today?"

Margie shrugged. "The usual teasing and name-calling. And no, Dad, I don't want you to come down there."

"But why can't I have some fun? I'd like to take that Cody Johnson dipstick and see how well he can swim underwater. With me holding his leg." John grinned wickedly.

"You'd have to take him pretty deep. He just had to show us all his talent. He can go to 30 feet tall."

"Wasn't he already the biggest kid in class?"

"Yeah. But I guess he wanted to be even bigger, so he could be even more of a complete butthead."

"That's often the way it is, Margie. But don't worry about it. He won't stretch that high too often; except when the JA assigns him to wash second-story windows, or repair telephone lines. And not even that in a strong wind."

"Why not?"

"Because his weight won't change. Mass always stays the same. Whatever he weighs normally is what he'll weigh when he stretches up. If he's 150 at six feet, he's 150 at thirty feet. It works in reverse, too. If somebody wants the ability to get real small, they'll still be 150, whether at six feet or six inches."

"Really? What about the people that fly? Don't they have to get lighter?"

"Nope. They just levitate themselves. Despite generations of study, science hasn't figured out how these changes happen, or how we become what we become or how we do what we do. The best that they've done is figure out how we can control what we become.

"No one is really aware of what's going on with their bodies during the change. We all just become some sort of super fluid under the shell, then change back into what looks like ourselves, but changed.

"When I was a little younger than you are now I decided I wanted to breathe and live underwater and on land—yeah, just like Aquaman. I concentrated on that for the last few months before I started making the shell. Everybody does it that way.

"That's why it's important for you to decide what you want pretty soon. You've got to have some time to concentrate on it, to align your mind, as it says in your biology textbook, so you come out with the ability you want."

One month later

"Whoa! Margie, thirds? Of course you have to eat a lot more to fuel yourself for the change, but aren't you overdoing it? You've been on a diet since sixth grade. Why the change?"

"Something you said, Dad. That our weight—our mass—doesn't change, no matter what we become. Well, I've decided. I did a lot of looking on the Internet. I'm going to do something that's only been done about a dozen times total over all these years. I'll be the first girl! It's pretty radical. But the heavier I am, the better it'll be."

"Really! Care to share?"

"Sorry, no. You and Mom can research it yourselves, or just be surprised." Margie, a young replica of her mother, allowed herself a secretive little smile. "Right along with a few other people."

"That's fine. It's your decision. Just remember the most important thing. Whatever you choose, make sure you can have fun for at least the next three years!"

Four months later

Margie sloughed off the last of the brittle green shell, stood up, and brushed herself off with a casual air. She looked exactly as she did when the shell enclosed her three months before. Her parents stood side-by-side, anxiously awaiting her first words. She smiled triumphantly. "Hi, Mom! Hi, Dad! What's for dinner?"

As custom required, they did not quiz her about her new self, and dinner was a quiet affair. Margie went to bed early. But that night, after her parents were asleep, she slipped into the backyard. She looked up at the sky, thin clouds skidding past the half moon. She took a deep breath and invoked her new talent.

An hour of experimentation later, she slipped back into bed. It was wonderful! It did feel very odd—her skin tingled, her ears tickled, her entire body felt stretched. But it did not hurt! She left her back yard and toured the whole town. She controlled it, and herself, completely. And, yes, it was *fun*.

She lay on her back in her bed and interlocked her fingers behind her head. She conjured an image in her mind, refined it, savored it, and set her lips into a satisfied smile.

At school the next day, while sitting in her seat, it did not take long for her tormentors to resume their self-assigned duties.

Cody Johnson appeared from behind her after "accidentally" popping her in the back of the head with his elbow, as usual. Margie found herself surrounded by Johnson and his three stooges.

"Hey, it's Large Marge the land-locked barge! Obviously you didn't decide to come out skinny!"

"Cody, James, Steven, Elmer, take your seats." They all looked up at Mr. Bradbury. He still faced the chalkboard, busily putting up the day's lesson. The three boys did not move.

"Now, boys!"

Reluctantly, Margie's tormentors took their seats. Mr. Bradbury watched them as he continued to apply chalk marks to the board. He possessed three-hundred-sixty degree vision all the time, which was one reason the JA decided he should be a teacher.

During lunch, Margie joined her best friends, Sandy and Brenda.

"You didn't call us," Sandy accused in a hurt tone. "We called you when we came out."

"So now you better tell us, Em. What can you do?"

As she started to answer, Cody and the Morons showed up. "Yeah, Margie the largie, what can you do? Float like a blimp? Bounce like a beach ball? Swim like a hippo?"

Margie smiled condescendingly. "If you want to know, Stretch, come to the park tonight and I'll show you."

Cody did not like being called "Stretch."

"In the park at night? Going to glow like the moon? I've got better things to do at night than go to the lame-ass park and watch you do something pathetic."

"Well, if you're scared of the dark, don't be. There are lights around that big grassy area. That's where I'll be. You'll miss something you've never seen before if you're too scared to show up. Your friends can hold your hands if that'll give you the nerve to walk in the park at eight o'clock at night."

Brenda spoke up. "We'll be there! Sandy and I aren't afraid of the dark! And I can't wait to see!"

Later, when they were alone, Margie told her friends, "Guys, what you'll see tonight is seriously rad. It's going to be scary. But you'll be safe. I promise. So don't freak out, okay?"

She arrived at the park well before eight o'clock. She stood beneath a cluster of big trees, hidden by the darkness, and practiced her new talent. It took only a couple of minutes to complete the process, and again assure herself of her control, and change back.

Margie was nervous, but not scared. She looked at the wide open expanse of grass just beyond the trees, illuminated softly by the tall lights installed on the perimeter. She saw them coming—Cody and his three friends, and her two best friends keeping several yards between themselves and the others.

Margie did not know for sure what would happen or even what she might do at the end.

When they were closer, she took a few steps toward them, then stood and waited for them to see her. Then she began.

She hoped her friends wouldn't freak. She didn't know how Cody

Johnson would react when he was attacked by a 160-pound wolf that had every reason to rip him to shreds. She conjured again the image of Cody Johnson on the ground crying like a little girl as her sharp white teeth and powerful slavering jaws opened inches from his throat while he wet his pants in terror.

She was sure of just one thing. This would be *fun*.

As the Crow Flies by C.M. Saunders [horror]

Three miles, they said.

As the crow flies.

Christopher felt he must have done at least half of that by now.

He was beginning to crest the mountain, booted feet thudding against the muddy path as he strode forward with purpose. It was cold up there. Exposed. The night was deathly still, and a light mist swirled around his lower half.

Overhead, the stars were out in force, shining so brightly it was almost possible to make out the lie of the path ahead. Below him, at the foot of the mountain, he could see the twinkling lights of the village.

"Be home before long...," he whispered to himself, thrusting his hands deeper inside his pockets and bowing his head. Great clouds of breath hung around his mouth.

Suddenly, a frown fell over Christopher's face, and the length of his stride shortened.

What was that?

Up ahead, was that a figure approaching?

Surely not, who would be treading these mountain paths at this late hour?

Somebody else like him, perhaps? Another lad who went for a few beers in a neighboring village, met a young lady, forgot the time and missed the last bus home. It probably happened all the time...

Then why was his goose-pimpled flesh crawling, seeming to writhe with a life of its own as it clung to his shivering bones?

The figure was closer now. Through the half-light Christopher could see that was, in fact, what it was. The looming outline of a man, dressed entirely in black, and wearing what looked like a hat.

He remembered the stories his grandfather told him when he was a kid. The stories about how the devil himself, the original fallen angel, stalked these mountainous peaks under cover of darkness, preying on weary travelers. Granddad never elaborated much on what he meant by "preying." He never had to. Christopher's imagination did the rest.

All his life, he had assumed Granddad must have been pulling his leg. Like the tall tales he often told about storming the Normandy beaches virtually single-handed. Christopher didn't believe in the devil. Didn't even believe in God.

But he had never walked these mountain paths alone after dark before, and right now anything seemed possible.

To his horror, Christopher realized that he had stopped dead in his tracks. His mind was racing. He felt like running. Should he turn around and retrace his steps? But where would he sleep tonight? He had to get home. Maybe he could just get off the path and hide until the figure passed. But that wouldn't work, either. If he could see the figure approaching, then the figure could certainly see him, too.

He glanced over his shoulder. Nobody there. He wasn't sure if that was a good thing or bad. He couldn't imagine what kind of people would be treading these paths after dark, but whatever character they possessed, they could be witnesses.

Witnesses to what?

Something was going to happen. Christopher could sense it. The atmosphere changed, turning more sinister and oppressive. The air around him seemed to crackle with electricity and there was not a sound to be heard. Even Mother Nature had fallen silent.

The approaching figure was now just feet away, but Christopher still could not make out any detail.

Strange; at this distance, even by starlight, he should be able to see some facial features.

He forced himself to move, put one foot in front of the other, as the world around him swam in and out of focus.

The next thing he knew; the figure was on the path just feet away. At such close range Christopher could now see the man was indeed wearing a hat and had a scarf wrapped around his face to keep out the night chill. He wore a long, black coat, with the collars turned up.

As they passed each other the stranger lifted a hand in

acknowledgement. Christopher nodded politely, then hurried on his way breathing a sigh of relief.

So, nothing sinister, after all. Just another tired traveler anxious to get home. Probably an ageing boozer making his way home from the pub.

He turned his head to watch the old fella stride over the crest of the mountain, and saw something that made his breath catch in his throat.

Dragging on the floor behind the man in black was a thick, sinewy tail. As Christopher watched, horrified, the tail flicked the air as if its owner was tasting it.

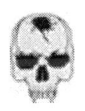

Yard Sell by Karin Fuller [horror]

I was driving fast when I spotted the sign tacked to a tree.

"YARD SELL."

Yard sales aren't my thing. From the day I could buy new, I did. But out here, there aren't shopping options. When I arranged this trip, I hadn't considered my occasional need for retail therapy.

I turned down a long-ago graveled drive—two ruts middled with grass deep enough to tickle my car's underbelly. Eventually, a farmhouse came into view, a two-story saltbox with an old metal roof and chickens in the yard.

Sawhorses with doors on top were set up in the yard. Typical yard sale junk—vases and crutches and out-of-style clothes—and praise the Lord! A table covered with books!

I stepped from my car, stooping to scratch the pair of dogs that tumbled over each other. The clap of a screen door caused me to look up. There, in farmer bib-alls, was a fine-looking man so tall his head near reached the top of the frame.

He walked toward me, friendly smile. Straight teeth. Square jaw. Messy mop of home-cut hair. There was an odd blankness to his expression that hid his age. He was either very clean shaven or hadn't begun growing whiskers.

He had gentle eyes. I didn't feel the least bit afraid.

Especially when he started clapping. And sort of hop-jumping.

"I thought no one was going to stop."

He extended his massive hand. Mine was swallowed by his. He shook longer and wilder than people normally do, but it was sweet. He was sweet. The world's biggest boy.

I relaxed.

"I'm Reggie."

"Anna," I said. "What are you selling here, Reggie?"

"Well, I'm not selling those dogs," his voice playful as he smiled at the homely pair. One dog had an overbite, the other an underbite. Both seemed undecided about whether they were short-haired or long, as there were patches of both. They were living, breathing cartoons. Ugly as hell.

"I'm more of a cat person," I said.

Reggie turned and raced for the porch, then reached into a box and began pulling out kittens, which he placed on his shoulders to retrieve even more. He was soon walking toward me wearing a circus of kittens.

He dropped first to his knees, and then sat. The kittens were having a time on their human playground, one sucking his earlobe while others whapped at his buttons. I plucked the ear-sucking calico from his shoulder and held her to me.

"Calicos are always female," Reggie said. "That's what Dad says. He's the smartest man in the world."

I was charmed by this man-boy, who I now saw had touches of gray in his hair. His face was completely unlined, save for a half-inch scar at his temple.

"Do you live here with your dad?"

His nod was much like his handshake—over the top.

"I was about to bring him outside when up you drove and out I came."

"You can get him while I shop," I said. "And leave this calico with me. I think I might need her."

While Reggie returned to the house, I headed for the books. I expected mildewed Reader's Digest Condensed, maybe some religious titles or books on farming or cars. Instead, I found titles on antimatter, quantum field theory, and particle physics—heavily notated and highlighted throughout.

I poked through a box on the ground. *Intracranial Surgical Techniques. Somatics: Reawakening Movement through Mind Control.* Many worn from repetitive reading, some with deeply crossed-out paragraphs and the word "BULLSHIT!" scrawled over the page.

I was anxious to meet the person who owned these books. I liked him already.

No matter what they cost, I had to have them, wanted evidence to back up the story I'd be telling friends about finding these books way out in Paradise, West Virginia, at the home of a handsome giant with the mind of a child.

I looked up and saw Reggie backing out the door with a wheelchair.

"Dad says I should offer you some tea," Reggie said.

"Tea would be wonderful."

I left the books to introduce myself. The resemblance was undeniable, but there was something more. He looked familiar. I tried to discreetly study his face, to mentally whittle away years that altered his looks and enabled anonymity.

He smiled.

"Have you figured it out? I can tell you're trying."

I smiled, then stared openly, as it seemed I'd been invited.

"You probably would've been in middle school, maybe elementary. And I wasn't in a chair then."

It was Nelson Risk! The youngest presidential advisor in history, before becoming a television personality. He'd been Hollywood handsome. Silver-tongued. Smooth. Nearly as famous for his womanizing as his wit. The person who inspired the creators of Ironman, Tony Stark.

"Give the girl a Kewpie doll. She has her answer."

"What's the Boy Wonder doing in the middle of nowhere?"

"Wonder Boy," he corrected. "It was just a dart at a map at a desperate time, and the only property for sale near the dart hole."

I suspected Reggie was likely the cause of his "desperate time," thought how difficult for the world's smartest to have a mentally-impaired child.

"This place suits us," Nelson said. "Been good for us."

We smiled as Reggie's singing carried out from inside. "This is how we stir the tea, stir the tea, stir the tea. This is how we stir the tea so early in the morning."

"You don't miss celebrity life?"

"Not at all. When you're famous for what's up here,"—he tapped his head— "the goal of most becomes to prove you aren't so smart. Your food choices are questioned. Doesn't he know chips are full of sodium? How smart could he be if that's what he eats? Every decision, regardless how minor, is critiqued. Clothing. Hairstyle. Women. Jobs I accepted. Advice I gave. And my mind never shut off."

I could relate. My brain routinely felt as if someone held its remote control and was flipping full speed through the channels.

"I graduated at 14," I said. "Wasn't a prodigy, though. Just motivated."

"And your motivation was…?"

"My dad is Shinehead."

Nelson laughed. "I've heard of him."

I wasn't surprised. The legend of Shinehead—homebrew distiller extraordinaire—endured. He'd headed a group of back-to-the-landers who built a compound a few ridges over. Barely renovated old buses, cobbled shacks. They grew their own and brewed their own and birthed their own babies. I'd been the first, consummated when Shinehead was 51 and Mom barely 15.

Shinehead got checks from the government. I never knew why, but at least five every month. Enough to support them and us kids, and their ever-changing collection of hangers-on.

Much as I loved Shinehead, I hated him, too. He infected every child—save for me—with a determination to never hold down a job. He schooled them in fraud, framing it as being clever enough to work the system.

Reggie banged through the door carrying three glasses of tea.

"Just talking to her about moving here," Nelson said. "Tell her how self-sufficient we are."

"We raise chickens and eat their eggs," Reggie said. "And I have a garden and fruit trees and cows. Dad has a deal with this man—every year he trades one of our cows for a whole bunch of meat, all wrapped in white paper."

Nelson winked.

"You should show Anna the pond," Nelson said. "Go for a walk. I can take care of any customers."

Reggie was so excited I couldn't say no. Soon, we were heading down a path, with Reggie bounding off to pluck flowers for me, often tearing them so close to the bloom there was nothing to hold, though I'd try.

"Girls love flowers," he said.

He took my free hand and pulled until we were running. I couldn't remember the last time I'd run.

When I slowed, Reggie looked concerned.

"I'm a little out of shape," I said.

"Your shape looks perfect to me." Reggie smiled, then he winked.

There was a flash of something in his eyes—there and gone—that chilled me, but then he was clap-hopping again, pointing to what looked like an old telephone pole with a basketball hoop jutting from the center of the pond. Several balls floated nearby.

"Dad put that up a long time ago, before he hurt himself."

"How did he hurt himself?"

Reggie plopped on his butt, began untying his sneakers.

"He didn't want to be sad anymore," Reggie said.

Nelson hadn't seemed like someone who would attempt suicide, especially with the responsibility of Reggie. He was lucky whatever he'd tried only left him disabled and didn't affect his brain.

"Our pond stays warm most all the time," Reggie said. "Never freezes, not even in winter."

"How's that possible?"

"A geothermal hot spring, I suspect," Reggie said. "Uncommon in these parts of the country, especially at this elevation, unless perhaps this isn't a mountain, but a volcano."

He tugged off his sock. His response was so oddly intelligent, but I supposed he'd heard his father's explanation enough times to memorize his response.

I dipped my foot in the pond—not bathwater, but close. When I turned to say so to him, I heard a splash.

His clothes were piled on the dock. Even his tighty-whiteys.

When he surfaced, he shook his head and swiped at his eyes.

"Come on!"

"I don't have a swimsuit."

"Neither do I. You don't need one."

He swam toward me, his breaststroke as athletic as any I'd seen.

"I promise I won't look." He turned his back. "Please? I have no one to swim with but the dogs, and they only just wade."

"And they probably can't shoot worth a darn."

"I like you. You're funny."

"I like you, too, Reggie. But I probably shouldn't swim naked with a man I just met."

He looked so pained I doubt I could've hurt him worse with a kick to the crotch.

"I'm not a bad man! I'm not!"

"I know."

"Then why won't you swim?"

I thought about that disconcerting wink and his strangely intelligent phrasing, and then met his gaze. It was as blankly hopeful as a Labrador when someone's holding a stick.

"Turn around. Don't look until you hear me in the water."

He turned. I disrobed. Standing naked on the dock, the cool breeze tickling my skin, was so instantly erotic that I felt dirty. Inappropriate.

I dove.

When I surfaced, Reggie lifted the basketball over his head and threw it toward the hoop, though we were too far away.

"Race you!"

I took off. Water had been my refuge for years. My apartment's indoor lap pool was open 24 hours. When sleep wouldn't come, I'd spend my nights mindlessly swimming.

Reggie still beat me to the ball. He aimed at the hoop and threw. Swoosh!

He swam to retrieve it. Shot again. Another perfect shot. Reggie was splash-bouncing the ball on the water. He threw it to me, and without thinking, I jumped to catch it.

Felt the cool air on my breasts.

Saw his expression.

Shit! He was so very much a boy, but also clearly a man.

He was striding toward me. The water was shallower here. I turned and threw the ball back toward the dock, then took off swimming toward it.

I'd almost reached it when I felt his hand grab my ankle. I yanked myself free from his grasp, but in doing so, took in a snoot full of water. I resurfaced coughing.

"You okay?" he asked. "I didn't mean to scare you."

"Fine." I coughed.

Reggie pointed at my chest.

"Do you have milk in those?"

Here I was thinking I was about to be assaulted, and he was looking at me as a cow. I shook my head no.

"Oh." He snatched the ball and threw it hard toward the net, and we were again racing after it. This time I won.

Soon, I was attempting shots without worrying about exposing myself. We were playing. I was playing. I couldn't remember the last time I'd played. Or hell—if I ever had.

Growing tired, I threw the ball toward the dock again. We swam easier this time, a slow-motion race. When we arrived, he turned his back without my having to ask and stayed turned until I'd dressed.

I retrieved my flowers and we walked back without talking. His goofy dogs spotted us and started trotting our way, tails wagging in circles.

Nelson waved from the porch, his large hand seemed a labor to lift. The kittens tumbled out of box. Reggie scooped my calico, kissed her on the nose, then handed her to me.

"I see you went for a swim," Nelson said.

I touched my wet hair.

"That water is amazing."

"It's a geothermal hot spring," Nelson said. "Uncommon in these parts of the country, especially at this elevation, unless perhaps this isn't a mountain, but a volcano."

I was struck by a swell of déjà vu.

"We played basketball!" Reggie said. "She shoots like a girl, but swims like a man."

"I'm so out of shape."

"Your shape looks perfect to me," Nelson said. Then he winked.

My stomach twisted.

"I'd better go," I said. "Have to stop and get some kitten supplies."

Reggie spotted a vase on the yard sale table.

"I'm gonna' fill this with water for your flowers!" He galloped back to the house.

"I appreciate you playing with him," Nelson said. "We used to have a great time together." He slapped the arms of his chair. "But I screwed that up."

We were beside the table of books.

"*Metaphysics. Language Patterns of the Mind.* This is some heavy reading."

He laughed. "And that was for fun."

"*Genetic Re-Engineering?*"

I flipped through the heavily-notated pages.

"I was such an arrogant ass when he was born," Nelson said. "Wanted him to be just like me. That's exactly what I got. Not a trace of his mother. He was my duplicate."

"In every way, save for one," I said.

Nelson shook his head.

"Every way," he said. "The older he got, the more like me he became. And just as unhappy."

Reggie bounded out the door.

"But I fixed that," Nelson said.

He was smiling sadly.

"Most sons want to be like their fathers," Nelson said. "Now, I'd give anything to be like my son. He was so happy after. But…"

He touched the scar at his own temple—identical to one I'd noticed on Reggie—then slapped the arms of his chair once again.

The book slipped from my hand. Nelson caught it, then handed it back.

"All I wanted was to be Reggie's playmate. I ended up being his burden instead."

Confused, I tried to collect my thoughts while pretending to read a page.

"These are amazing books," I finally said. "Any idea what you want for them?"

"You'll have to ask Reggie," Nelson said. "They're his."

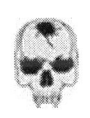

Spruce by Kolin Gates [horror]

The sky was overcast, distorting the panorama of the Rocky Mountains in the distance. I stretched my arms high overhead, feeling my hair tickle my lower back. If there were any people around, I didn't see them through the thick trees. There was a little clearing where the cabin sat, but green firs and white birch trunks crowded in from all sides, making for a peaceful hideaway.

I've always loved the winter. Since my boyfriend felt the same, it was an easy choice to opt for a winter vacation instead of suffering a sweltering road trip. Also, the fact that it was the winter season meant that we only had to pay half price.

Standing outside in the bracing cold in a bra and sweatpants was invigorating.

A fog was curled around the distant mountaintops. It circled their swells and pressed against them like a living thing. From my position higher up, I could see the peaks above the fog as it filled the valleys below. Snaking around the trees near the cabin, some of the wispy outrunners of the main body were shifting and pulsing. I was beginning to really feel the cold when I heard the door open behind me.

I smiled as Jake encircled me with his arms, hugging his chest against my shoulders. He pawed my bra for a second, then wrapped a blanket around me.

"It's really pretty out here."

I nodded and rubbed his forearms, glad for his warmth.

"What do you want to do today?"

"I was thinking we could make coffee and breakfast, then spend some time in front of the fire," I said, pressing my ass against him. He pushed back and snuggled me closer.

"That sounds good," he said.

I was about to turn and lead him inside when an elk pushed through two drooping evergreens. The dusting of January snow rattled off the branches as the massive elk walked into the clearing. He raised a bushy face and looked right at us. The sharp antlers on his head were a lighter brown, matching his flanks. He shook them and snorted at us, black eyes rolling in a face full of shaggy, dark brown hair.

"Wow, I've never seen a wild animal this close," I whispered.

Jake's arms squeezed a bit harder, as if the sound of my voice surprised him.

"He looks pissed, we should go inside," Jake said, starting to pull me back.

The elk jerked his head to the side and stamped the ground.

We began to back away slowly. I had only walked to the edge of the patio, which was six feet from the kitchen door. The elk opened its mouth and let out a weird, high-pitched scream. From an animal so large, it seemed utterly out of place. The screeching trumpet wail stopped us both.

I clutched the blanket around my neck and shoulders, wondering why the elk would scream like that. We hadn't read the wildlife brochures from the visitor's center. Then the elk spun around and lowered his head.

Silent and sinuous, at least ten big wolves appeared, crouching for a moment. They bared teeth, little puffs of frost smoke clouding their faces. Then they attacked.

The elk slammed his antlers into one of the darting wolves, then kicked back and struck another. The wolf it kicked flew through the air, landing in a broken, whimpering pile. Then the wolves were upon him, and they mercilessly ripped into the elk's flesh. The largest wolf wrapped its powerful jaws around the elk's throat, bearing it down. Sharp teeth flashed as their muzzles became red. I'd never seen something like this in person and the violence was shocking. It was like the most disgusting part of a zombie movie, where the zombies begin eating a living person.

The wolves clamored over the mewling animal, shaking their heads from side to side. Jake pulled me back, into the kitchen. I couldn't stop staring, and as Jake was shutting the door, my eyes locked with the largest wolf's. His big yellow orbs were intelligent and cruel, and I felt that they read my soul to the base terror that had overcome my body. It smiled, gore dripping from the canine jaws.

Brown wood snapped in front of my eyes and broke the contact.

"What the fuck! I thought they said there might be bears, but not wolves!"

Jake was pacing the kitchen, looking out of the window at the grisly scene in the clearing.

I couldn't talk, but I thought that wishing for bears when you already had wolves seemed borderline crazy. When Jake crouched down next to me, I realized that I was trembling and shaking. Something visceral had been shocked deep within me, some animal instinct from ages past when humans had been hunted like that elk. I had always thought humans were predators, but now I realized that they could just as easily become prey.

"It's ok, baby," Jake said, stroking my hair. "It's ok, don't worry. They'll drag him away and leave us alone soon."

But they didn't.

The scratching began again.

I shivered and gripped my walking stick, hugging the length of wood against my stomach. The wolves were out there, in the dark, scratching at the doors. Jake was pacing again. He had freaked out in the afternoon, when we realized that our phones didn't have service, and the cabin's phone wasn't working either. They had told us that the lines went down sometimes in the snow.

The solitude that I had blessed yesterday morning had become a nightmare.

Standing outside in my bra had felt so liberating and powerful. Now, hours later and with no one walking past except the eight bloodstained wolves, I felt anything but powerful.

The overcast had turned to snow in late afternoon, and as the dark side of twilight approached, the skies were heavy with white flakes. The wolves had spent the afternoon dismembering the elk and dragging the pieces to various points around the cabin. We watched them from the windows as they laid down and tore into the meal like they hadn't eaten in weeks. When they had stripped the bones, the alpha sniffed at the wolf who had been kicked in the fight. Once he set in on him, the others joined, and they'd soon devoured the corpse. I hadn't seen them find the other one who had been speared by the elk's antlers, but I assumed that it had suffered the same fate.

"What do they want?" Jake asked for the hundredth time. "Do they just want out of the cold?"

"No, Jake. They want to fucking *eat* us."

He glared at me, but gripped his walking stick so hard that I saw his knuckles turn white.

Jake had duct-taped kitchen knives to the sticks, making ugly spears out of them. We'd bought them as a joke, not really expecting to do much hiking. Neither of us felt like doing what we had expected to be doing. The scratching never stopped.

"Hey, get away from there!"

Jake was shouting at the kitchen window. I turned to see the bright yellow eyes of the alpha. His huge head was cocked as he watched Jake shaking his spear from the living room. I thought it seemed like a dismissive motion when the big paws fell away from the window and the wolf disappeared back into the night.

I heard some growling outside, coming from the side of the cabin closest to me. There wasn't a window on that side, just a fireplace in the corner and a long staircase leading up to the balcony overlook. We had a fire going and the popping of logs initially distracted me from the sound.

"Jake, what is that?"

He paused his pacing and listened, cocking his head like the wolf had done.

"I don't…"

The lights went out.

Jake's eyes were huge in the glow of the fire, now the only illumination in the room. A thud and a snapping sound came from outside. Jake frowned.

"Did you see a fuse box or anything like that?"

I shook my head.

"Put another log on the fire. We need some light to find candles or flashlights. They've got to have something around here."

I put another log on. "Jake, there are only ten left."

"Ten what?"

"Pieces of firewood," I said.

"So?"

"So, where are the others?"

"Oh," he said. "Oh."

"Yeah."

I remembered seeing those. They were lined up outside on the back patio, under the overhanging balcony. With the wolves.

"Here's some candles at least," Jake said, rummaging under the kitchen sink.

"What about our phone flashlights?"

"Oh! Good idea, Emily," Jake said, walking back to me.

I smiled at his praise, forgetting our situation for a moment. My phone was still at seventy-five percent, and if I dimmed the screen a lot, it would probably last for a while. Plus, I wouldn't use the flashlight unless I absolutely had to. I put it in my pocket.

Jake lit two of the four big candles, white cylinders the size of mason jars. He came and sat down next to me, lifting the corner of my heavy blanket to slide in. We held hands in the warmth, our free hands keeping hold on the walking sticks. Minutes passed, and as the little flames of the candles jumped and danced, the scratching continued, and Jake's breathing became slow and regular. I was trying to stay awake, but I didn't want to get up and disturb him.

The first thing that I noticed when I woke up was that the scratching had stopped.

I shifted against Jake's bulk and opened my eyes. Standing before the couch, was the big alpha wolf. It was silent, eyes slitted as it stood there, waiting for something. I moved the blanket away from my legs. My right hand was still on the walking stick, and my left was still in Jake's.

The cabin's front door was ajar, black night and white snow streaming into the living room. I squeezed Jake's hand, hard.

He woke up slowly, not jerking awake like I had feared. The wolf stood there, like a stuffed animal in a country restaurant. I felt Jake tense and I knew that he was awake and had seen the animal. In the doorway, I saw more wolves stalking outside, looking in on the big leader. The wolf growled low, moving for the first time since I had awoken.

It tensed, dropping a few inches as its weight shifted back onto its hind legs.

"Run!"

Jake's shout surprised me and I wasn't ready when he thrust his spear.

The wolf was, and it dodged aside smoothly, fast and fluid. It opened a red-stained mouth and lunged. Jake screamed, thumping the butt of his stick against the wolf's back. I stabbed at the alpha but his eyes rolled up to me and he moved, his jaws still locked onto Jake's forearm.

The wolf let go suddenly and leapt up onto Jake's chest, his teeth champing down on the side of his neck. When it jerked its head back, blood sprayed out in a fan. I screamed and ran for the bedrooms.

The hallway was dark and I sensed the other wolves gliding into the cabin behind me. By feel, I pushed through the door on the left and slammed it shut. I had lost my weapon, but I felt my cell phone in my pocket. As I pulled it out, I heard scratching at the door behind me.

No Service.

My chest felt like it would explode. I thought that I must be hyperventilating. My index finger trembled as I dragged my thumb up the screen and pressed the little flashlight icon.

The bedroom lit up in a sickly, white glow.

I saw the bed first, then something caught my attention. Over at the window, the blinds were open. I shined my light at the window and bright canine eyes winked back at me. I spun to the other window and saw another wolf, patiently watching.

It was then that I noticed my sobbing was overpowering the

scratching at the door. But when my chest hitched to take big gulps of air to continue the involuntary crying, I heard it.

The scratching, and a new, ripping sound.

Something wet, gurgling through the little crack in the door.

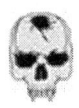

Peach Cobbler by Lisa Finch [horror]

Mirabelle's hands fished in the hot soapy water for another dirty dish. She'd really let them pile up this time.

Yet it was impossible for her to stress over the little things when her hands were soaking in water. It had always been that way. Was it like that for everyone?

Water brought out her dreamy side. Like right now, she mused, as she looked out into the clouds. They parted in the sky, just for her. A sign. She knew she stood at the edge of a new chapter in her life.

A whole new life. And she knew just how to celebrate.

She took a whiff of the peach cobbler baking in the oven. Tonight at supper she'd feasted on her favorite foods, and now she'd finish it off with her favorite dessert.

And she'd have the whole weekend to herself!

Wilfred would've hated every last thing she'd cooked today. Shepherd's pie, red cabbage, stuffed peppers. She'd even had salad with Thousand Island dressing, a thing Wilfred detested. He'd have pulled a face at seeing it on the table, so she rarely bought it.

He'd have frowned on all those dirty dishes.

She shrugged. Well, he wasn't there to order her around for once. As she washed another plate, she reflected that she'd been bossed her whole life. First her mama and papa, then her five older brothers and sisters. When her mama had birthed Mirabelle's little sister, Tessa, she'd thought at last she, Mirabelle, could call the shots.

But the baby was colicky and screamed all the live-long day. Mirabelle had been the one to mostly mind her little sister; it had seemed a cruel trick that even an infant could be so demanding.

When Tessa died two months later, Mirabelle was at first relieved that she was gone. But when she saw how her mama's shoulders drooped from that day on, sometimes Mirabelle would stand at the empty cradle and a sick wave of nothing-will-ever-be-right again came over her. No one knew why the baby died. Sometimes Mirabelle wondered if she had just wished it so.

Now she sighed and watched the clouds chase each other. She turned her focus back to the sink where the hot water had turned her hands all puffy and pink, her left ring finger bare and strange.

She could hardly remember a time without Wilfred. She'd met him at age sixteen, gotten pregnant, and had to marry him. Next thing she knew, they had six children.

She'd spent her whole life under someone's thumb. But now, things would be different. Yes sirree, come Monday morning, things would be as different as could be.

Her bags were packed; she was ready. It would be on her terms for once. No more Wilfred dictating every little thing. No more children and grandchildren relying on her for everything. They'd have to look out for themselves now.

She thought about the one other time she'd had a few days of freedom, so sweet, like eating a whole stick of cotton candy all at once.

But that delicious freedom had carried sadness with it: her dad had died, and she'd taken the train to be with her mother for the funeral. Wilfred had minded the children.

The night before she left to come back home, her mama had cried and said she hated to see Mirabelle go. Mirabelle had cried too, and she kept on crying, all the way back on the train.

Even now, she felt a lump rise in her throat and brushed away tears with the unsoapy back of her hand.

She wouldn't think about that. Just about the weekend ahead. She'd watch anything she liked on the TV, she'd read a book cover to cover, she'd put her feet up. She'd let the phone go to answering machine. She wouldn't do one lick of housework and not even any more dishes. These would be the last.

The dishes now dripping in the rack, Mirabelle dried her hands and pulled the cobbler out of the oven. She'd have a huge dollop of vanilla ice cream on the side. She could almost taste it, creamy and cold wedged against the hot, bubbly peach dessert. And after that, she'd have one or two of those vodka slushies she'd seen in a woman's magazine her neighbor had finished reading. They'd sounded so good, and today she'd finally made some, just for herself. Oh, she knew what kind of reputation people got who drank alone. But who would know?

"And anyway, Mirabelle," she said to herself in the empty kitchen, "who gives a shit?"

But first, the cobbler. Golden brown and bubbly; she pulled it from the oven and let it rest on the stove top.

She opened the freezer for the ice cream and nearly jumped a foot.

"Sweet Jesus, Wilfred!" She put her hand on her pounding heart. "I forgot I put you here. Should've put you in the basement freezer. Geez."

She avoided looking at his lifeless eyes, moved his frozen severed head aside, and found the tub of French vanilla ice cream, her favorite.

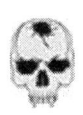

The Seeds of Foundation by Pedro Iniguez [sci-fi]

Theo walked in the building and felt a little embarrassed. It was a clean, immaculate room with white tile floors and chrome walls. He wore his cleanest white shirt and only pair of slacks. He had polished his shoes shortly before coming. Working construction, he never really needed to look presentable, but today was different.

The room was full of professional men and women speaking into earpieces or at their desks face-to-face with customers. A man in a perfectly pressed suit approached him with an even more presentable smile. Theo extended his hand, "Hi, I'm Theo Martinez. I called earlier."

"Ah, yes," the suited man said. "I'm Michael Braun, I spoke to you. Let's walk to my office where we can speak privately."

They walked past offices with people carrying on whispered conversations. A muted television set played a news segment about the second wave of explorers arriving on Mars. They came to a room in the back. Michael Braun bowed his head and waved his hand at the door. Theo entered and sat down.

"Now, Mr. Martinez, we can speak."

A framed picture of Braun's family stared back at Theo: two girls no older than five, and a wife with a smile as attractive as her husband's.

"My father came to this country," Theo sighed, "when borders were more than walls on a line. They were a game of Russian roulette. If you didn't die in the desert, or drown crossing the river, you were jumped by drug traffickers or shot by angry ranchers."

Braun reached for a manila folder that read 'Burial Services' on it, probably having heard the same story time and time again.

Theo continued, "He raised me in this country alone. My mother left us before I was old enough to remember her face. He did everything to ensure I had a stable living condition. If I didn't achieve success in school, it's only because of my failures, not his as a father." He looked down and took a breath. "He is getting old now."

Braun pressed his lips together and nodded his head, the universal display of 'Yes, I understand.'

"But the worst thing is, Mr. Braun, that he doesn't remember who I am."

Braun looked confused.

"He has Alzheimer's. My creator doesn't recognize his only creation." Theo's eyes became moist. He took a deep breath and forced a smile. "Anyway, I wanted to be ready and give him a proper send-off when the time comes."

"Of course," said Braun. He opened the manila folder. "And we have a slew of great options based on your…financial circumstances. Now, our burials are–"

"I don't want him buried, Mr. Braun. Not exactly."

"I see. We do offer cremation services, and they are, in fact, not as costly."

"No, I was thinking something a little closer to my heart. My father was a gardener, you see. It was the only job he could get here without papers. He would make other people's lawns look perfect, only to come home to a lawn-less backhouse. He had huge concrete hands, but he was always so delicate with flowers. Then I heard about the Rebirth Program. It's perfect. A service that sends loved ones to Mars, with an assortment of seeds in a bio-degradable coffin, a little something to speed up the terraforming going on there."

"Mr. Martinez, the Rebirth Program has a very steep price tag. And a rather long waiting list."

"I don't have a family," Theo said, picking up Braun's family portrait. "I've been saving up just for this. It's the least I can do. He crossed borders to sow the seeds of my foundation. I think it's only proper that he continues doing the same for future generations."

Braun nodded and put the manila folder back. He rifled through his drawer and retrieved a blue folder. "Go home and read over these papers and bring them back to me signed, and we can begin the process of shipping procedures, coffin selection, and if you'd like to pick a flower arrangement…"

Theo got up and shook Braun's hand. "He is the flowers."

"You really love your father," said Braun.

"And I always will," said Theo. "He's the best dad in the whole world."

Old-Fashioned by H. A. Titus [sci-fi]

Ninety percent of people who have an alarm system never activate it, Chase Yolander included. Despite the iridescent security chips visible in the windows, the office door alarm hadn't been wired into the space yacht's system.

It was a good bet that the safe wasn't armed, either. Still, better careful than caught. Penny pulled the door closed behind her and turned to look around the room. Xerc already stood in front of the wall safe, holding a framed Monet.

"Not very clever, hiding it behind a valuable painting." Penny took the painting from Xerc. The dim overhead lights made the warm, swirled paint colors glow.

"Real?" he asked.

"Very."

"Don't suppose we can take it?"

"I can't exactly slip a Monet into my shapewear."

Xerc's green eyes flicked to her, a grin spreading lazily across his face. "A painting-shaped lump would definitely detract from that dress."

Penny raised an eyebrow, and a smile tugged the corners of her lips. "For shame, Archley. And you call yourself a professional."

He smirked and turned back to the safe. His black-gloved fingers danced over the surface. "As professional as you are old-fashioned, my dear."

She stepped closer and examined the shiny box. It was flush with the wall, which was straight since the interior office didn't have the curve of the ship's outer walls. The safe looked old, with a spin dial in the middle and gold flourishes framing the edges of the door. A keyhole, scarcely large enough for a pin, sat beneath the dial.

Xerc tapped his lower lip. "There's no need for a keyhole *and* a dial. Not to mention the fingerprint scanner." He nodded to the little pressure pad that sat below the keyhole.

She'd missed that. The pad was nearly the same glossy black as the rest of the safe.

Penny stopped herself from running her fingers through her loose curls. The fewer hair strands and skin cells left for InterPol to find, the better.

Why would someone have three ways to get into a safe? All their intel said Yolander wasn't *that* paranoid. Perhaps two of the locks were decoys.

As Xerc continued examining the safe, Penny looked around the office. The Monet had been the only picture in the room. What little wall space wasn't covered in bookshelves was paneled in dark wood. It was probably even real. She sniffed. The smell of lemons and linseed oil lingered in the room. Definitely real wood polish, at least. It didn't have the zest of chemicals that usually underlined canned smells.

There was no sign of a projector, which meant Yolander didn't use a holo-computer in this room. And the books. Yolander had a fortune in hard-backed volumes crammed onto the shelves. Penny stepped up to a shelf, ran a finger along the creased spine of a novel, then eased it from the shelf. Some of the pages looked dog-eared. She smiled. Not just for show then.

The title and author were embossed in gold on the red cover. *The Secret Passage* by R. C. Morgan.

Xerc began humming to himself. Penny looked at him. He pulled his glass tablet phone from an inner pocket in his tuxedo jacket and tapped a sequence into the home screen, which turned the screen dark. As he held the tablet up to the safe, Penny looked over his shoulder. Tiny green lines appeared on the tablet screen, indicating wiring that connected to the dial, print scanner, and keyhole.

She felt Xerc stiffen, and chills circled Penny's wrists like invisible handcuffs. She took a deep, steadying breath. Somewhere, their intel had been wrong. Yolander did indeed use alarms.

"Good thing I didn't try picking the lock," Xerc muttered, replacing the tablet in his pocket. "Should've brought the decoder and not listened to that twit in Exion."

"Smuggling *that* bulky beast in would have been more impossible than stealing the Monet," Penny said.

Xerc shrugged. "See if the books are worth anything." He moved to the immaculate marble-topped desk. "I don't want to walk away without something to show for it."

Penny went back to the shelves and pulled another book free. Another R. C. Morgan, *Of Gates and Grottos*. Something tweaked at the back of Penny's mind.

Old-fashioned. Penny pulled another book from the shelves and checked the title page. And another. And a third, all from different parts of the room. All of them were old Gothic novels and pulp adventure stories, stuffed with secret tunnels and hidden passageways and forgotten treasure.

She carried them across the room to where Xerc was rifling through the desk and put them in front of him.

"Valuable?" he asked.

"I don't know. They're reprints of old pulp fiction from the early nineteen-hundreds. I doubt they even exist as tab-books. He probably had them specialty printed." She waved her hand around the room. "Everything in here is designed to look old and classy. Based on the books and the look of the room, I think there's a way into that safe. We just need to find it without setting off the alarm."

Xerc raised an eyebrow. "You sure?"

She licked her lips. "Ninety percent."

"Good enough." He ran his hands over the carvings on the desk's sides.

Penny scanned the room. There, in the corner by the door. The chair cushion sagged, and the side table had a few water rings staining the finish, unlike the pristine surface of the other tables in the room.

She slid past the chair. Her eyes caught one title halfway down the right side of the case, a slightly tattered-looking volume titled *The Secret Key*. She grinned and gave the book a sharp tug. A click sounded, and the safe door swung silently open.

Xerc bounded across to it and reached inside.

"Anything good?" Penny asked as she stepped up to his side.

"Oh yeah." Xerc removed a necklace. A deep-blue diamond glittered from the middle of the pendant, outclassing the stones that surrounded it. His grin made the corners of his eyes crinkle as he held it up against her neck. "Old-fashioned, indeed."

And Now, Fill Her In by Jamie Gilman Kress [fantasy]

As the plane rose steadily into the sky, water vapor streaked up the glass like tears in reverse. Kiya, her head resting on the cool plastic near the pane, swore she heard the movement of the rivulet—a dry slither, like a snake through dry summer glass.

A trick of her imagination; impossible to hear anything over the rumbling of the giant engines. She liked that about flying. The isolation. Thirty thousand feet from everything, the world hidden behind a shield of fluffy white cotton clouds. Only the other passengers in existence, and each of them pigeonholed into assigned seats and lost in their dreams or books or vacant thoughts. Every person a microcosm of their own, and none of them touching Kiya, a realm onto herself.

Her eyes fluttered closed, mind drowsy with the reverberations of technology singing through her bones. She drifted.

Children, dark with summer sun and woodland adventure dirt, trampled through the kitchen, all three loud, hungry, grinning. A woman, older, blonde, smiled back, handed them each a sandwich thick with peanut butter and leaking gobs of apple jelly.

The man sat at the table, reviewing tables of numbers on a tablet, oblivious to the domestic bliss happening all around him. From the tablet holding his attention came the harsh bleeping of an alarm. A small pop-up box: Leave for Airport.

He rose, straightened his tie, gave the woman a perfunctory kiss. Never even bothered to say good-bye to the kids.

But then, he only planned to be gone two days. How could he know he'd never see them again?

Kiya jerked, not awake—she'd have needed to be asleep for that—but aware. Her eyes flitted about the cabin against her volition, searching out the thing she desperately wanted not to find.

And Now, Fill Her In

He sat in the aisle seat four rows ahead, face only partially visible, but enough to recognize, to know. He'd be dead before daybreak tomorrow.

Kiya always considered flying her sanctuary, the one place the fragments of others' lives failed to find her. And now, she'd lost even that small reprieve. But why?

The lump in her throat solid, she swallowed hard to dislodge it. She needed to figure this out; it must be important. But before she even finished the thought, her head lolled, came to a stop propped again near the window. Her eyes fluttered closed.

Sunlight tinted pink by the gauzy curtains poured over the face of a boy with the soft rounded features of youth. A strong jaw, regal nose—he'd be stunning once he matured.

The woman wore her years well. At least twice as many as the teen in her bed, beauty had been softened by time, rubbed soft and comfortable. Until you looked into her eyes. There the years showed, the time hard, cutting glass. Her gaze was pure envy when she glanced once at the sleeping boy before slipping out of his arms and into the bathroom.

Just another conquest. She'd be out of the city before his parents found him, before he realized he'd been abandoned.

She felt nothing as the motel room door clicked shut behind her.

This time when Kiya jerked back to herself, her bony elbow caught the book held by the man beside her, sent it spiraling. She barely noticed as she cast about in a frenzy.

There, a few rows behind, on the other side of the aisle. The woman wore a silk blouse and dark brown slacks. She looked normal, bored.

Kiya knew better. Recognized the predator eyes.

People tried to fill the emptiness within them all sorts of ways, and Kiya had witnessed many: work, drugs, sex. But, she'd never before been linked to someone so *empty*.

It left her feeling cold to the core.

"Hey," spoke the man beside her, book forgotten at his feet, "are you okay?"

For a moment, Kiya just blinked at the stranger, unable to process his words, to recognize he meant them for her. Then, with a sharp shake of her head, the fuzz cleared. "Fine," Kiya croaked, then swallowed. "I'm fine. Thank you."

The man, pudgy with kind, watery blue eyes and only a puffy ring of dirty snow hair, looked unconvinced, but after a brief pause where his eyes never left her face, he retrieved his book and retreated within its pages.

Kiya released a soft sigh, closed her eyes to relieve the headache building, and once again floated away, carried like a leaf trapped in a stream along the lives of others.

The man with the book sat in a recliner, old but well cared for, with a purring cat in his lap. The cat, a circle of marmalade contentment, looked up once and blinked its pumpkin eyes before returning to its slumber.

"Do you think it will work this time?" The voice, female, came from someone out of frame. However, even without visual cues, the tone, all restrained hope and tangling resignation, made the speaker's view clear.

The man spoke, his hands deftly stroking the cat, "She's asking for help. It's a step. We have to try."

A small woman, her hands frail and a-twitter like dancing birds, became visible. "I know, but I wish..." she trailed off, one hand coming to rest briefly on the man's shoulder. "You hate flying."

He caught her fleeing limb, kissed her palm, his eyes tender and gentle. "I'll bring a book. I love you, Carmen."

"I love you too, Eric."

Kiya finally understood.

Turning in her seat, she looked at the man, at Eric, until he felt her gaze and put down the book.

"Something wrong?" Rather than annoyed at her intrusion, he seemed concerned. "You need me to call an attendant?"

And Now, Fill Her In

Kiya wished she'd introduced herself before, exchanged pleasantries, given some small part of herself, if only her name, to this man. Made some connection, no matter how brief to someone so truly *good*.

She'd seen so much pain, so many unappreciated, shallow lives, but she'd never touched someone like this: a man who deserved to be honored, who should not be allowed to fade from the tapestry of the world.

Throat like a vice around the words she wished to speak, she awkwardly reached out a hand, rested it against his cheek. His memories flooded her: Katherine, the child lost, but finally ready to get help; Carmen, the wife he'd loved since grade school and won over in college; the friends and family and jobs, and pets, of a man who lived life well and graciously.

The images swept through her like a brook overflowing its banks, washed away her own darker memories.

No one had ever loved Kiya, the strange girl left on a doorstep, raised by a long line of strangers. Even grown, she'd found creating true relationships hard, drifted through lives on the currents of other people's experiences. Clung to the unsavory moments of the soon-to-be-dead because she'd failed to make strong memories of her own.

As hollow in her own way as the woman in the silk blouse.

Kiya felt no fear despite what must be coming. She knew, felt deep in her bones that her spot, this particular seat among the many, would be spared. If she stayed here, in this place, she'd survive the plane crash, go on about her simple, cursory life.

Or, she might make a different choice, create a ripple that mattered.

Eric still watched her, confusion furrowing his brow. He made no move to shake off Kiya's touch. "Miss," he said, worry darkening his eyes, "if you need help—"

"Change places with me, please."

"What?" He continued to watch her with concern. "If you're sick, I can—"

"No," Kiya said, struggling against the rising tide of another vision. "Just a nervous flier. Being near the window's making it worse."

"Ah." He smiled, compassion and humor replacing the anxiety. "No problem."

He rose swiftly, helped her up as they swapped places. Once she'd settled in, he rested a hand on her arm, the contact comforting and brief like a cool summer wind. "Is that better?"

Kiya felt it, a shift in the currents of the visions battering her to be seen. Among them now, she'd find herself. "Much. Thank you, Eric."

"How—" he started, but the question became a gasp and then a scream as the plane began to plummet.

Kiya closed her eyes and gave in, let herself be dragged down by the undertow of her final vision. And found peace.

The Gravedigger by Liam Hogan [horror]

There's a sharp ring of metal against...what? A gravestone? A coffin?

I jerk upright, listening over the moan of the wind. Then I'm out of my cot, reaching for the greatcoat slung across the back of the wicker chair, stooping to lift the army rifle from the bench. It's been a while since I've had to chase grave robbers from these grounds. Once, it was my reputation as a marksman that stayed them from their sordid task, now...now there are other concerns and the risks far outweigh the meager rewards.

As I ease the door of the gatehouse open, cold air whistles in, ruffling the folds of my unbuttoned coat. From the depths of the dark room behind me, a sudden voice commands: "Wait."

I turn and level the rifle at the slim figure that steps into the slanted rectangle of bright moonlight. So, I realize, that I might see him more clearly.

"You must give them longer," he says, ignoring the firearm aimed at his midriff. "It will take them some time."

The ringing is louder now that the door is open; a metallic beat over the familiar anguished howls. "Zombies?" I ask, certain already of the answer.

His lips purse in distaste. "This is 1913, Mr. Sanger, not the dark days of primitive superstition. They are not the undead. Never were, and, perhaps, never will be."

I feel my grip tighten on the stock of the Lee-Enfield and ease a finger towards the safety. "What are they doing out there?"

"Merely digging up one of their own. You buried Elizabeth Marshall today, did you not?"

"I did," I reply, defiantly.

"In chains and under concrete?"

"Yes."

"Then as I said, it will take them a while to release her from her binds. They are not, alas, as coordinated as you or I, Mr. Sanger."

I stare at him, standing there, once again making free with my name. "And you are?"

He laughs. "Forgive my rudeness. I should have introduced myself. But then, I doubt you would be willing to shake my hand. Perhaps a lowering of that rifle will serve instead?"

I keep the rifle where it is. "You are one of them?"

He tilts his head slightly to one side. "If you like. They—*we*—are not all simple beasts. It depends on the exact progression of the virus. In some, indeed in most cases, it causes a rapid swelling of the brain, leading to coma and permanent damage to all but the most basic functions: the need to eat, the fear of pain, a desire for the company of their own kind. In others, the effects are less severe. They retain a basic level of intelligence, the ability to understand commands, a distorted and painful memory of what they once were. In rare cases, such as mine, the patient retains all the capacity for thought they ever had and gains much more besides."

"Gains? What gains?"

"Come, Mr. Sanger. You have seen enough to know the answer to that. Immortality! Or as close as we are ever likely to get." He takes a step forward, the rifle all but forgotten, daring me to disbelieve him. "Strange, is it not? Something medical experts have sought with such passion down the ages; how vehement their reaction against it, against us! They should be working to cure the unfortunate side-effects, rather than trying to eradicate the disease, rather than trying to destroy the afflicted. I'd hardly call that standing by their sacred oaths, would you?"

"The...afflicted are classed as legally dead," I observe, neutrally.

"And yet unlike others of your increasingly numerous profession, who separate the head from the neck, burying it at the corpse's feet, or who rush to cremate the comatose, you choose the infinitely more laborious method of internment. Why is that, Mr. Sanger?"

Is this why I am still alive? Is this the riddle that stays his hand, that stops him from killing me in my sleep?

"I am a gravedigger," I reply. "It is not my place to pass judgement on those I bury. Merely to ensure that once buried, they stay buried. Hence the chains, hence the concrete. My usual precautions in these troubled times."

He raises an eyebrow. "You do not approve of what my friends are doing out there?"

"No, I do not. Let no one say I do not do my solemn duty without the due care and diligence it deserves."

"Don't worry," he says, "they will fill in the grave once they are done."

"That," I reply, grimly, "is hardly the point."

"Is it not?" he muses. "Then perhaps we can save each other some effort in future. The people you are burying, they are not dead. If the bodies were not interred with such indecent haste, you would have evidence of that for yourself. But the law dictates that once some ill-informed quack unable or unwilling to detect the frail pulse of someone in a coma signs the notice of decease, then the services of a gravedigger must be employed. Very well. Employ them we shall. But if the coffin were empty?"

"I do not think the reverend—"

"The reverend will join our ranks by this time tomorrow," he says. "The bandage he wore on his arm this afternoon covers a nasty bite. One he well deserved, Mr. Sanger. He is not as respectful of the dead, or the living, as you are."

I take in this startling news. "May God rest his soul."

The moonlit figure tuts. "You forget. He is not dead. He will not die. And though God has nothing to do with it, I, a mere mortal, may yet influence his fate. Decide if he should retain his faculties, or join those unfortunates he lacked the compassion to pray for and who are incapable of praying for themselves."

"And how would you go about that?" I ask, intrigued. "How do you play at being God?"

He ignores my jibe. "I was a medical man, before. I would be again, given the chance. Prompt action is required. Ice! Cooling the body reduces the swelling of the brain, prevents the injury it causes before the virus puts a stop to apoptosis."

I look at him blankly. "I don't—"

There's a pause, a moment of silence, from both within the gatehouse and without. Then the ringing begins again, erratic now.

"*Apoptosis*, the Greek for falling away. What your cells are programmed to do, Mr. Sanger, when damaged, when attacked. It is not the lack of oxygen, the invasion by a virus, or the cold grip of winter that kills. It is the cells themselves, choosing to die. An imperfect and outdated process, surpassed by modern science and one which this virus arrests.

"If you shoot me, you will do physical damage. You will destroy a small number of cells directly in the path of the bullet. A few thousands, at most. Maybe a million. But why should the death of so few cells lead to the death of the whole? Even if for a while there is no blood reaching my lungs, my brain, why should these organs not spring back to life the moment oxygen-rich blood does reach them? That is the blessing of this virus. One no doubt it employs for purely selfish reasons, protecting its host to guarantee its survival, its spread."

"God's will—" I mutter, but again he swiftly interrupts.

"Is tuberculosis God's will? Is cholera? If so, then this virus is also his will and it is the duty of all who have the capacity of thought to treat the infected with respect. And yet, the country convulses with fear, with hate! There is little I can do about that, Mr. Sanger. The number of us who, like me, can discourse rationally, who might argue our case, is few. So, I ask for your help. And knowing that those you bury are not dead, how can you carry on as before? How can you still claim to be a reputable man?"

I bristle at that, this stranger in the night passing judgement on me, on my profession. If I were to let fly the bullets in my rifle, no court would convict me; to them, I would be shooting a dead man.

I think for a moment. His intent is obvious. He aims to hold me here, by talking, while the foul creatures in the graveyard go about their mindless business. He aims to allay my fears by allowing me to train my rifle on him. I wonder if it is even still loaded; how silently he must have crept into my room! If he wanted to dispatch me, he has already had plenty of opportunity.

"You understand," I say, "I cannot be seen to—"

"Do not worry. We will be discreet. And when the time comes— *if* your time comes—we will move Heaven and Earth to make sure that you yourself are treated with the utmost care."

I shudder, a reaction that amuses him.

"Come," he says, "lower your weapon. Go back to sleep, if you can. We will be gone well before sunrise and you may consider this night a bad dream. In the morning, when the reverend falls ill, you will offer to take over the duties of laying him and other unfortunates to rest. You will order in supplies of ice; money will be provided. And you will leave me a set of keys to the Chapel of Rest."

He takes a step forward, his eyes trained on me, and another step, until the barrel of the rifle is a hand's width from his waistcoat. I lower the weapon, though I keep my hands firmly on it. "What will you, and your companions, do?" I ask. "You will never be accepted here."

"Even when we outnumber the uninfected?" He smiles. "But you are right. We will leave these lands. There is a turmoil in Europe, the death throes of imperialistic empires. There will be war, Mr. Sanger. A war unlike any seen before. A war that cries out for a race of men less prone to injury, less fearful of death. Our war. We will prove our worth on the battlefields."

I look on him in renewed horror. I saw action in the second Boer War, learned my trade there, and though this doctor claims to be a rational man, I find his posturing more frightening than even the thought of his lumbering friends out in the graveyard.

"Do you really think you are so indestructible?" I ask. "Have you no weaknesses at all?"

A cloud darkens his countenance, whether cast by my scornful tone, or perhaps I had chanced upon a sore spot, I could not tell.

"Medicine will catch up. There is already a cure for syphilis and more will surely follow. Science will conquer all of the ills, Mr. Sanger, even influenza! Even, perhaps, the virus that gifts us immortality. But then, why would we want to do that?"

There's a peal of staccato thunder as five metal shells drop to the floor around his feet, and my finger convulses on the trigger of the empty rifle. When I look up again he is at the door, staring at me with those eyes, those very distinctive eyes.

"Now, if you'll excuse me, I need to attend to poor Lizzie. The woman you buried alive today is my sister. Did I mention that?"

He steps backwards into the night.

"I do hope she's not in too bad a state, Mr. Sanger. I really do. For your sake."

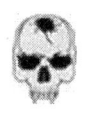

How Earth Narrowly Escaped an Invasion from Space by Alex Shvartsman [sci-fi]

Lieutenant-Admiral Whiskers stared at the ominous planet on his view screen. It was still very far away, a tiny fishbowl with an even smaller moon hanging at its side like a saucer of milk. The view grew steadily clearer as the invasion fleet approached its target.

The sound of the war council entering the room broke his reverie. Whiskers turned and stood at attention as a pride of elderly felines shuffled in. They wheezed as they struggled to climb into the seats placed around a long oval table. Whiskers thought it ironic that not a single one of them was in shape to hunt their own dinner, and yet this bunch of fat cats led the expeditionary force that had conquered over a hundred worlds.

Last into the room was an enormous tuxedo cat. Chairman Meow, Supreme Commander of the Armada, regally carried his nearly thirty pounds of flesh into the swiveling chair at the head of the table.

"You may commence with your report," said Admiral Smudge.

Whiskers nodded to the adjutant, who dragged in a holographic projector and pressed his paw against the touchscreen. An image of a blue and white world sprung to life.

"This is Earth," said Whiskers. "The only planet to have successfully thwarted our invasion attempts in the past."

There was a murmur among the council. "Impossible!" shouted one of the cats. "The Armada has never known defeat in its five-thousand–year history." He banged his paw against the table.

"I didn't say we were defeated," said Whiskers, "merely thwarted. The natives of this world are cleverer than they look. Observe." Whiskers displayed a holo-image of huge ape-like creatures using ropes and tree logs to move a stone slab the size of the conference room.

"Earth was among the first planets colonized in the early days of the Armada," said Whiskers. "It was an easy conquest; the natives worshipped our ancestors as gods." He displayed an image of a gargantuan cat statue resting in front of an even larger pyramid structure. "But something went terribly wrong. A small colonial force left behind to govern the planet gradually lost their technology and even their intelligence, little by little, with each passing generation. A terrible native drug they call *catnip* may be to blame."

Whiskers waited until another round of murmurs had played itself out. "When the Armada returned to this sector of space and our hails went unanswered, I authorized a small scout force to investigate.

"They landed on Mars, the next planet over, and studied the broadcast signals from Earth. That was when they discovered the terrible truth: countless descendants of our people are living on Earth as mindless beasts. They are kept as pets by the natives."

The sounds of protest were thunderous this time. "This can't stand," declared Chairman Meow. "We shall decimate these apes and liberate our cousins."

"Indeed," said Whiskers. "However, there is a complication." He changed the holo-image again, to display a landscape full of skyscrapers spread out as far as the eye could see. "The natives must've learned much from the technology left behind by our ancestors. They have grown numerous and scientifically advanced. We can defeat them, but not without risking an unacceptable level of casualties.

"The scout team, which studied the natives extensively, suggested a propaganda campaign instead. The apes welcomed us as gods once; with a little nudge, we might persuade them to do it again."

"Were they successful?" The ears of Information Minister Snowball perked up at the mention of the tactic.

"They were doing well, but the apes must've discovered their plan and retaliated," said Whiskers. "Under the guise of scientific research, they launched something called the Curiosity Rover. It landed squarely on top of the advance team's base, crushing everyone inside."

Smudge dug his claws into the table surface in anger. "You mean to tell us the natives used this Curiosity to kill the—"

"Nine lives were lost, yes," said Whiskers somberly.

"All the more reason to crush the apes," said Smudge.

"That was my initial reaction as well," said Whiskers. "However, the apes must have been really threatened by the scout team's propaganda work to launch a counterstrike. Isn't that reason enough to continue their efforts?"

"How?" asked Snowball.

"The apes are fond of spending a lot of time perusing a planet-wide patchwork of information networks they call social media," said Whiskers. "The scouts infiltrated these networks to insert text and images that would bring the public opinion about cats to an all-time high. Soon, apes will not be able to resist us. Kindly examine your displays."

A two-dimensional touchscreen activated in front of each of the cats. They browsed through the images, translations overlaid over the Earth language text.

"Fascinating," said Snowball. "I must say, this cat really is quite long."

"And this one truly is grumpy," said Chairman Meow. "Yet thousands of these...humans, is it...claim to like him."

"I find the challenge of expressing my thoughts in under 140 characters strangely appealing," said another councilor.

The cats continued to browse. One by one, a number of friend requests popped up on Whiskers' own screen.

"I am adjourning this meeting," said Chairman Meow, his eyes never leaving the screen. "We need to study this social media phenomenon in greater detail. Also, I have to figure out how to plant these virtual vegetables with maximum efficiency."

On the following morning, Whiskers woke up to find a brand new social network software on his computer, programmed in the cats' own language and with accounts pre-generated for all the senior staff.

"I must give credit where it's due," posted Chairman Meow. "This human invention is a far more efficient method of communicating than constant in-person meetings." There were a dozen likes on this post.

"You know, the human cubs are actually kind of cute," posted Snowball. He attached a photo of a plump baby with big blue eyes, and an overlaid caption that read "I can haz bawl of milk?" In the comments, somebody linked to a video and wrote: "A species that came up with Top Cat can't be all that bad."

Another commenter added: "Some of their beloved cultural icons are named after us. Cat Stevens. Cat Rambo. Tiger Woods."

Whiskers scrolled down, past the status updates and game requests and pictures of the crew's breakfast, until he reached another post by Chairman Meow.

"I have decided not to invade this planet, for now," it said. "At least not until we find out which faction wins the Game of Thrones."

There were many likes under this post.

That is how Earth narrowly escaped an invasion by the great cat armada. Oblivious to how close they came to the threat of annihilation, humans continued to generate amusing content on the Internet, including but not limited to Game of Thrones episodes, cat memes, and science fiction short stories that make fun of them.

And somewhere in outer space, felines are sharing funny human pictures on Catbook.

Hard to Swallow by Nick Nafpliotis [horror]

When most people hold a pill in their hand, it represents some manner of impending relief. Whether it's prescription strength meds or a good old-fashioned, over-the-counter pain reliever, swallowing that little pellet is supposed to do something that will make you generally feel better. Hell, even the bad stuff that you're not supposed to take is all for the sake of acquiring some badly desired short-term benefits for your brain and body.

But for me, this pill represents something that will wreak all types of havoc on my heart whether I take it or not. This is the old "red pill/blue pill" scenario, only both options are attached to varying degrees of nobility and suffering.

If I take this pill, like I did diligently a couple months ago, then I finally get to be a normal, functioning member of society. Sure, I might be the guy who causes folks on the subway to look over their shoulder more than once. But I can live with that if it also means I get to wake up in the morning, go to work, come home, and go to bed like everyone else. If that type life comes with friends and the potential to actually talk with people other than my shrink, I'll gladly take that as well.

The real benefit to it all, however, would be the added storage space. As it stands right now, the cutting equipment alone is taking up the entire basement. Once you add in the bones and hanging frames for each one, I can barely move down there. Sixteen bodies doesn't sound like a lot at first, but people come in all different shapes and sizes. There's no standard way to set and arrange them all in the proper positions without utilizing a large amount of square footage, most of which is taken up with the arms and legs jutting out from the torso in whatever stance The Rattler tells me to put them.

I learned long ago not to argue when The Rattler tells me to do something. It's best just to make the offering, clean off the flesh, bleach the bones, and put everything just the way he wants it. Otherwise, the screaming between my ears gets so loud that it feels like my eyes are going to pop. Procuring and preparing the offerings is fairly gruesome business, but I know that it needs to be done.

I also know, however, that I've been pretty damn lucky so far. This isn't like the serial killer shows on TV where some suave psycho keeps up a normal life while hacking away at fleshy versions of his own personal demons. I know that if I keep this up for much longer, I'm going to get caught...which honestly didn't matter that much until I met Liz.

The Rattler had told me to bring him someone with her build and features, so I figured it was my lucky night when she sat next to me on the subway home. You can imagine my surprise, then, when she started talking to me like we had known each other for years. Hearing voices, seeing things move inside the walls, food coming to life and trying to eat you first...she'd been through all of it. I couldn't tell initially if she had to procure offerings like I did (there's no casual way to ask about something like that), but I was pretty sure she didn't. Her master had been an addiction to drugs and some fairly unsavory work, all of which she now claimed to have left in the past.

As we continued to talk, I purposefully ignored my stop. After making the entire loop three times, it became clear that she had done the same. I also noticed, after observing her as more than just another mark, that Liz was absolutely stunning. She was short, with huge brown eyes and short black hair that she let fall right above her shoulders. Her tan skin framed a muscular build, which indicated someone who could hold her own in a fight and took care of herself a hell of a lot better than I did.

Seeing Liz like that was the first time in forever that I'd noticed another human being in a way other than just making cold, calculated observations at The Rattler's behest. It felt strange to be attracted to someone again...and even stranger to suspect that the feeling was reciprocated. As we got off the train that evening, she gave me her number without me even having to ask.

This is the point in the story where I expected some sort of cliché commandment by The Rattler to kill the woman I had grown too fond of. I wouldn't have done it, but the impending confrontation and subsequent torture was not something that I was looking forward to. To my surprise however, He didn't really seem to mind at all. As long as I was still out there procuring his offerings, He couldn't really care less if I had a girlfriend or not.

Things between me and Liz started off well and got better from there. I kept waiting for the other shoe to drop, but it never did. Instead, we got closer and closer to the point that I shared pretty much everything with her (except for the stuff I had to do for The Rattler, of course). At every point where I expected her to figure out that I was crazy and kick me to the curb, she ended up either being completely understanding or even more crazy herself.

I'll never forget the day that I met Liz's mom for the first time. I worried that the meeting would be an entire evening at Olive Garden filled with bread sticks and judgment. It was, but not for me. Liz's mom berated her incessantly about various things to the point that the awkwardness was numbing. To Liz's credit, however, she handled every barb and quip with aplomb.

My favorite part was when her mom went on a rant about Liz having fake boobs. I, of course, was completely fine with it. My policy has always been that if they exist on this plane of reality, then they're real. But Liz's mom seemed to think it indicated some sort of deep-seeded flaw in her daughter's character.

"You were born beautiful," she'd said while slurping up some type of awful-smelling lemon soup. "Why do you have to ruin your body like that?"

"Whatever...I love my bionic enhancements," Liz responded with that beautiful little half smile of hers. "In fact, I want my next one to be a robotic arm with a shoulder-mounted laser like the one in 'Predator.'"

Yep, this woman was pretty much perfect for me...which also made me want to stop working for The Rattler. I didn't want to go to jail for the rest of my life or be executed (depending on which state found out about me first). I just wanted to be with Liz.

As you might imagine, The Rattler was not very pleased about my new outlook on life. But I was determined to do things my own way for once. As the screaming blared in my ears, I made an appointment with a shrink. It was absolute torture at first, but to the guy's credit, he called BS on enough stuff I was saying that it became apparent he was actually listening. After diagnosing me with a slew of disorders (some of which I didn't even realize existed), he prescribed an anti-psychotic, which I began taking immediately.

In the beginning, it was perfect. The voices were still there, but they'd gone from a deafening roar to barely being a whisper. I no longer felt like I had to find offerings for The Rattler, either. I could wake up, go to work, come home, spend the evening with Liz, and repeat the beautifully perfect and normal cycle day after day.

After two months, however, I noticed something: Liz wasn't making any sense. At first, I figured that maybe it was just one of her little obsessive phases she had, only this time about something that I didn't understand. But after weeks of trying to decipher what sounded like complete gibberish coming from her mouth, I started to realize that it was me who was changing. By the fourth month, I had gone from being blissfully happy whenever she was around to feeling completely repulsed by her mere presence.

Making things worse was the fact that Liz could feel it, too. She would cry and scream and ask why I didn't love her anymore. Despite how cold my feelings had grown towards her, it still killed me to see her like that. My heart may have not felt like it had before, but I still remembered what it was like when we were madly in love with each other.

So I stopped taking my medicine. I also stopped going to my shrink. With every voice mail and text message from him that I deleted, I could feel The Rattler slowly easing back into my life...along with that small fire in my heart for Liz lighting back up again.

It took a while for us to reconcile. At first, she didn't want to get anywhere near me out of the fear that I would break her heart again. Hearing her say that now with so much more clarity hurt more than any physical pain that I've ever experienced in my life. But after a month or so of talking to each other again, she could tell that I was listening to her like I'd used to, hanging on every word and taking them in like wine into a glass. I understood her again. I loved her again.

And unfortunately, I also had to start working for The Rattler again. Despite my best efforts at resisting His call, I had no choice to but start filling the orders…which meant that someday, probably very soon, I was going to get caught.

So here I am, standing in front of this mirror, covered in bleach and blood while holding the pill that can make it all stop. No more offerings for The Rattler…no more Liz. Either they remain a part of my life together or I turn my back on them both.

I've weighed the decision, so has The Rattler, and so have you. What will I do?

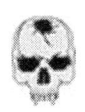

The End of the World is, Like, So Boring by Amy Sisson [sci-fi]

I am getting, like, so tired of talking to myself. So I'm going to record this and post it later—that is, if my stupid phone doesn't keep spazzing out on me.

It's been a day and a half, and nobody is answering my texts or calls, not even Alison, and that's just weird. My mother isn't answering either, but that's her. Last year she disappeared for a whole week, and it turned out she'd gotten married in Vegas. It was no biggie, though, because she had it annulled. She said it was the most fun, because the guy was young and hot, so it proved she's still got it.

So anyway, on Friday my mom said she was going to a party at some producer's mansion down in the Valley. The housekeeper has Friday nights off, so I texted Alison to see if she wanted to sleep over, but she had to spend the weekend at her dad's. So then I texted Janey, and she said sure. When she got here, she said we should invite Cooper and Gage to hang out, because Cooper is hella gorgeous and Gage isn't bad either. Oops, I probably shouldn't put that part online. I'll take it out before I post.

Then Janey dared me to call, but I made her do it because she called dibs on Cooper, so why should I do her any favors? It took twenty minutes for Janey to work up her nerve and I was getting totally bored, but she finally called Cooper, and then Cooper called Gage to check, and then Cooper called us back and said yes, but we forgot to give him the address so he had to text us for that a few minutes later.

Then we only had an hour to get ready. Janey was bummed because she said she looked like a cow, but we're almost the same size so I lent her my green halter top. Which, note to Janey, I want that halter top back, and you can keep Cooper. I'm starting to think this is all his fault, anyway.

When the guys finally got here, I gave them the grand tour. They thought the rec room was the shit, but they could've cared less about my mom's walk-in closet, which was Janey's favorite part. When the guys saw the hot tub on the terrace, Cooper was all hey! we should go in. So I asked Janey if she wanted to, and she was all sure, if you lend me a bathing suit. The guys elbowed each other and said what about them, so Janey rolled her eyes and said duh, underwear!

So we found some Mike's Lemonade in the mini-fridge on the terrace and then got into the hot tub. Gage kept kicking me and pretending it was an accident. Cooper was telling Janey about this new app his father's been developing, AllFriendz he called it, where you connect all of your friends on their phones and then it automatically connects their friends, and their friends, so you get like the biggest live network all at once. I said what if your friends block the request? and he said it had ways to get around that. He said it would be bigger than Facebook, and Janey was like, so? Facebook is for old people.

So Cooper grabbed my phone from the edge of the hot tub, and he and Gage fiddled with it *forever*. Me and Janey got tired of being ignored so we talked about maybe going shopping the next day, because that new Coach store in the Galleria is supposed to be open by now. It'll probably have all the same stuff as every other Coach store, but you never know.

A zillion years later, Cooper was finally ready and said we would be witnesses for the first live test of AllFriendz. I was like, is your dad gonna be okay with this? and Cooper said if he wasn't, he should've used a better password. Then he hit "go" on my phone and handed it to me, and the rest of their phones all rang at once, but right when that happened Gage kicked me again and I dropped my phone in the water. I felt this little electric shock and I thought my eyes were closed for just a second, but I must've passed out for a few minutes because the next thing I knew, all three of them were gone, the jerks. I felt around under the water until I found my phone and fished it out, and then I was like oh shit. The case, which is supposed to be waterproof and I am *so* going to take it back and complain, had this crack in it, and the picture was sort of jumping around. So I turned it off and yelled for Janey.

When they didn't come back, I got out of the hot tub and sat there shivering because now I was cold, so I yelled again and said ha ha, I'm not playing hide and seek and btw, I could have drowned so thanks for nothing. But they still didn't come back, so even though I was mad I started looking for them in my mom's closet and the rec room and everywhere else. Cooper's car was still in the driveway so I knew they couldn't have gone far but I was like whatever, and I went to my room to put my phone in the Ziploc with rice I keep in my dresser. Okay, so it wasn't the first time I dropped my phone in water. At least I've never dropped it in the toilet like Alison did that one time.

Finally, I was like screw them, and I went downstairs and raided my mom's liquor cabinet. She doesn't know I know where the key is, plus I never take too much from any one bottle, except that one time Janey and Alison slept over and we drank an entire bottle of vodka, and I had to pay one of the gardeners fifty bucks to replace it before my mom noticed. Oh crap, I better cut that out too, before I post.

Anyway, I tried some vodka mixed with cranapple juice, but I could barely taste the vodka so I put more in, and then I could taste it too much, so I added some orange juice. And then more vodka because I was still pissed at Janey and the guys. I just lay there on the couch thinking about the angry texts I was going to send to Janey once my phone dried out, and before I knew it, it was the next morning and I had a major headache and this disgusting taste in my mouth.

I looked out the front windows and saw Cooper's car, so I searched the whole house *again*. That made my head hurt worse, so I went and got one of the Vicodin my mom had left over from her last "spa treatment," aka facelift, but don't tell her I said that. That made me sleepy again and I crashed for a couple of hours.

When I woke up, I remembered my phone, so I ran to my room and *thank God* it turned on! But after it powered up, I realized it was acting kind of weird. My call log showed 1,413 outgoing calls, all at the same time that Cooper did that stupid friends thing. Anyway, I sent Janey a text right away saying this really isn't funny anymore, but she didn't answer.

And the day keeps getting worse! Since Cooper's car is here they must have walked somewhere, but the only place you can walk if a few of the neighbors' houses, and it's not like we know them. And I just realized that the housekeeper never came back. She has Friday night and all day Saturday off, but she's live-in, so she's usually back by dinnertime. Where the hell is she?

Oh crap, my phone is flickering again. Hopefully it just needs to charge. I'll come back and finish this later.

Okay, I'm starting to get a little freaked out because now it's Sunday morning and I've tried calling *everyone* I know and *nobody* is answering their phones. Seriously, I tried my friends, my mom like twenty times, my dad, my stepmom, my mom's lawyer…no matter who I call, it just rings and rings, and nobody is answering my texts. So I finally walked to two of the neighbors' houses, but nobody answered the buzzers and I can't climb the security gates.

Hang on, I hear something.

OMG, that was my mom's *landline*. I forgot she even had it! It was Aunt Carol, my mom's half-sister, the one who lives out on that farm in Kansas where my mom made me spend two whole weeks back when she and my dad were getting divorced. I was like, Aunt Carol, I don't know *what* is happening, and she said that when she drove into town for some groceries last night, she couldn't find anybody. She said she went into a diner, but it was empty with half-eaten meals on the tables. She used the diner's phone to call the police, but she couldn't even get them, and finally she decided to go check on her closest neighbor, Martha, who's like four miles away from her farm. She found Martha and her baby at home, and Martha was trying to call everyone *she* knew. So Aunt Carol brought the two of them back to her farm, and then she got her address book, a paper one I mean, and found the old number to my mom's house here.

Aunt Carol made me tell her everything that happened starting on Friday, and then she said since I was okay, she needed to hang up and check on some things, but she promised to call me back in a few hours no matter what. I didn't want her to go because I could tell she was getting scared too. She said to lock all the doors and make sure I had candles and a can opener ready in case the electricity went out. I said why would it go out? and she said it was just in case and not to argue. She said I should fill the bathtubs with water too. I don't know why but at least it'll give me something to do. We have a lot of bathtubs.

So the five hours 'til Aunt Carol called again were the longest of my life, but the next few days are gonna be even worse. Aunt Carol is on her way to California with Martha and the baby and two other people she managed to find. She said since I can't drive yet they would come to me, and we'd all be better off here where it's warmer anyway. She also said they would call me from along the way whenever they could find landlines. I was like, Aunt Carol, just give me your cell so I can call you, and she said honey, we don't *have* cell phones, don't you get it? That's why we're still here. So I said well *I* have a cell and *I'm* still here and she said that there must be some reason I wasn't affected. I said affected by what? and she just sighed and said they had to get on the road and we'd figure it out once she's here.

So now that's all I've been thinking about it and I just don't get it. What does this have to do with cell phones? And seriously, what kind of people don't carry cells anyway? I mean, everyone is connected, that's what Cooper was trying to prove with that stupid app he put on my phone.

But anyway, I hope Aunt Carol and her friends get here soon. I think it's gonna be another long night.

Peppermint Tea in Electronic Limbo by DJ Cockburn [sci-fi]

Ray Marken could have sworn the tiles surrounding the hospital room were the whitest things he had ever seen until he saw the teeth of a rep who had just closed a sale. Her smile shone down on him, pinning him to the bed. A biometric reader appeared in the rep's hand so fast Ray did not even see where it came from.

He reached up to take the reader and scan his retina. The sleeve of the hospital gown slid down his arm. The rep glanced at the blue patch of a tattoo, faded beyond all recognition. Ray tried to remember what it had been. Things often slipped his mind these days. Not that it mattered, when the prostate cancer would kill him long before his mind went.

He pressed his thumbs to the reader to complete the transaction. "There, if I'm accepted, Afterlife Inc. will receive my full estate to hold in trust for the maintenance of the servers."

Nothing wrong with his mind when it mattered.

He met the rep's eyes. She would be the last human he would ever see and he wanted some kind of connection with the girl, but his gaze skidded off her professional smile. He sighed. She was on the upside of fifty, which he guessed made her a girl to a ninety-nine-year-old man.

"Thank you, sir," she said. "Now if you'll just keep still…"

Keeping still was about the only thing Ray's body did well, so he did it while she placed the helmet over his head. Green lights flashed in her spectacles and he recognized one of the new eyeball tracking systems.

The girl's eyes refocused on Ray. "We're connected," she said. "Remember what we said? You'll feel a bit funny at first, but you'll be in the interview room almost straight away."

"Cool."

Her smile bathed Ray in indulgence. Who said "cool" anymore? She closed the faceplate. Ray's senses switched off.

Pain vanished.

Losing his constant companion was so disorienting that it took a moment to realize he could not sense the bed. He did not even know which way was up.

An unfamiliar sensation made him flinch. It felt somehow human, although it engaged none of his five senses.

Hold it together! The command bellowed from within himself, but he had no idea where. A life in middle management gave little experience of barked commands.

The human sensation returned. He forced himself to relax into it. There was something reassuring about it, he realized. The echo of the command subsided. Edges began to form in darkness. The sensation resolved into a voice. "It's okay, Ray. Don't panic."

The voice was reedy but reassuring, like the voice of the oncologist who had told Ray he had a few weeks to live.

A light in the darkness became a window. A rectangular block became a coffee table. A dark mass became a sofa behind it. White-painted walls solidified around him.

"Can you see me, Ray?"

Ray did not see where the middle-aged man had come from, but he belonged perfectly in the suburban living room, right down to his paunch. His long-sleeved shirt looked comfortable, as though it was his idea of casual attire.

"Ah good, you're resolving nicely," said the man. "Please have a seat."

He gestured at an armchair and Ray sat down without really knowing how he did it.

"It takes the brain a few moments to interpret the signals, but you seem to be adjusting well. You were warned, I take it?"

"The rep just said I'd feel a bit funny."

"Oh dear, that was rather an understatement, wasn't it? I suggest a cup of herbal tea. It usually helps."

"Tea? How?"

The man settled himself on the sofa and waved at a teapot that Ray did not remember seeing before.

"Peppermint or chamomile?"

Ray blinked, gathering his thoughts. "Peppermint, please."

"Excellent choice." The man poured from the teapot and handed Ray a cup without placing a bag in it. Ray tested it with his lips, but the tea was just the right temperature and tasted of peppermint.

"Good," said the man. "It helps to engage all the senses as soon as possible. Now we can get started. My name is Pete. I'm the doorman for today."

"You're doing the interview?"

"Well, yes, we have our formalities. Though this is a little more than a formality, if you follow."

Ray placed the cup on the saucer. Something looked wrong. He looked down sharply. His hand was a blur with a few finger joints.

"Don't be alarmed," said Pete. "Your self-image is taking some time to form, but it's quite normal."

"My self-image?"

"Let's just say that you won't want to look in a mirror for a while. Not to worry, I'm sure you'll harden out in a few moments. Shall we begin?"

Ray nodded.

"That door," Pete pointed behind Ray, "is the door to Afterlife. If you go through it, this model of your consciousness will be uploaded to Afterlife's servers and you'll join us in, well," Pete gave a deprecating chuckle, "immortality, really."

Ray turned to see an ordinary white plywood door. There was no keyhole in the handle, and the wood looked too soft to hold the screws of a bolt very firmly. Ray felt a flash of contempt for anyone who would depend on such a fragile barrier. But then, he thought, it wasn't a real door so it wouldn't need a real lock. He turned back to Pete and took a sip of tea.

"Would you believe that some people have tried to break down the door?" Pete shook his head. "I must admit; we like to make a little test of it."

"A test?"

"You've seen our brochure, of course, but you can't begin to understand how Afterlife works until you've been at least this far. Our emotions are not contained by our bodies, as in prelife."

Ray felt his lips twitch. "Prelife."

"Well, yes, in our bodies. We have to be careful who we let in. People prone to anger, people carrying any sort of unresolved angst, even people with poor social skills…well, you have to keep in mind that a consciousness only functions if it's continuous. Backing it up just doesn't work, so any sort of disruption could make the cat among the pigeons seem rather benign."

"That must limit Afterlife's intake."

"Very much so. You might call us a rather exclusive club. Of course, you wouldn't have got this far if your records had shown any obvious problems. You were born in nineteen fifty, so you'll be in good company. The technology came at just the right time for the last of us Baby Boomers. You went to Pennsylvania State College, sixty-nine to seventy-two. You weren't drafted?"

Ray remembered typing his final dissertation on an ancient PC that had been top of the range at the time. He was conscious of something about the memory that did not quite add up, but he concentrated on Pete.

"No, my number didn't come up."

"Then you went into human resource management?"

"My whole working life."

Ray remembered filing cabinets giving way to servers as his hair receded. He tried to remember further back, but the memories would not come. Instead, he vaguely remembered stilted buildings burning to the sound of helicopter rotors. His mind flinched from the odd image. It must have been a movie he'd seen once.

"Married of course," said Pete.

"Yes, for fifty-four years."

"But not until you were forty. A little late, perhaps?"

Ray remembered Mary laughing as they counted the wrinkles on each other's bodies. "Worth the wait."

"A happy marriage, then?"

"Oh yes."

"Good, marital troubles are hard to leave behind. Now I have to ask you this, and I hope you won't be offended. How do you feel about her being rejected by Afterlife?"

A blur of emotions flickered through Ray. He remembered sitting by Mary's bedside, holding her hand as he watched her eyes close for the last time.

He took another sip of tea. "I had the chance to say goodbye to her properly. I'm just happy with that."

Pete nodded. "Some men might feel some bitterness. If you'd had some idea of spending eternity together, it must have hurt to be refused?"

Ray met Pete's gaze. "No, Afterlife was a new idea at the time and we hadn't thought that far ahead. Anyway, I'm not given to strong emotions."

An image of a gun aimed at the back of a kneeling man's head flashed through Ray's mind. The gun did not waver as it blew pieces of skull and brain in all directions. Ray could not remember where the image came from. He had never liked violent movies.

Pete smiled. "Excellent. You seem to have coped very well with losing your wife. Are there any other sources of trauma in your past? Particularly painful bereavements? Episodes of depression? Harrowing experiences?"

As Pete spoke, Ray felt something probing his reactions that had nothing to do with Pete's gaze. He summoned memories of suited men and women shuffling papers or tapping keys. He became aware of an itch in his memory rather like an incipient sneeze. If he ignored the urge to sneeze at an embarrassing moment, it usually went away. The technique seemed to work as a post-human.

Pete sat back and smiled. "Yes, we've all had our altercations with the helpdesk, but it hardly scars us for life."

An image through the eyes of a man lying on his back, vision blurred by drugs and pain, leapt into Ray's mind. He somehow remembered the movie was about a man being interrogated for the location of Mujahedeen commanders in Afghanistan and that he had seen it in 1987, but he could not remember whether it was on television or in a theater. A man in the image threw a switch and dissolved the memory with a white flash.

Ray focused on Pete's smile. "I think I can manage not to strangle any IT support people I run into in Afterlife."

"Good to hear that. I see your self-image is developing nicely."

Ray held up a hand. The outline was indistinct, but he could no longer see through it.

"I think we've covered everything," said Pete. "You'll find the door unlocked if you try it. Some people like to have a last look at prelife, but it's entirely up to you."

A thrill of excitement simmered through Ray's sense of calm. He drained the cup of tea and stood up. "No, I think I'm quite ready."

"Then welcome to Afterlife. Please do remember what I said about keeping emotions under control. It takes some practice, but it becomes second nature after a while."

Pete opened the door and stood aside. Ray stepped on to a lawn. People milled around tables covered by print cloths and plates of finger food.

An overweight man smiled and held out a plate. "Are you a newcomer? Please join us. Would you care for a cucumber sandwich?"

Ray looked around him. This was Afterlife? A bunch of fat people at a garden party? The sandwich tasted as bland as cucumber sandwiches did in reality. Other people turned toward him, and Ray found himself the center of attention.

"Now now," said the man with the sandwich plate, "let's not crowd our new friend. We all felt a bit odd for the first hour or two."

He turned back to Ray. "Please do try a vegetable kebab. It's not as though we're in danger of running out. Ah, I see your hands are almost complete. That's excellent. It will be nice to know if you see yourself as fat and middle aged as the rest of us."

People laughed as though they had heard the quip before but still appreciated it.

Ray held up his hands and narrowed his eyes at the scarred knuckles and plain gold wedding band.

"I must say, I was rather disappointed," the fat man was still talking. "I'd been warned, but I still rather hoped to find myself looking like, oh I don't know, Bruce Willis in *Die Hard* or someone else *thin*."

That brought another laugh, which Ray heard as though from a great distance. The sneeze-like itch was back, and Ray felt no need to ignore it.

"Oh really, Charles," said a woman. "You talk such nonsense. Wasn't life so much more comfortable when you stopped fighting the waistline and settled into middle age? I don't think any of us would have got through the door if we hadn't felt that. Besides, I might have risked my marriage with, what was that Englishman's name? Hugh Grant. But Bruce Willis? Please!"

Ray was vaguely aware of attention slipping away from him as he remembered the face of the man he had once called Lieutenant, now as creased as his own. He couldn't understand how he had forgotten meeting him, only a few days ago.

"Know why they washed her out, Marken?" the memory of the Lieutenant's voice was sharp and clear. "She'd picked up too much of your trauma. You probably didn't talk about it much, but she felt your pain and made it her own."

Ray chewed the kebab. What trauma had he been talking about? Ray had spent his life in a happy marriage with an undemanding job. So how had he known a man named Lieutenant?

"They won't touch any of the guys or anyone close to us," the Lieutenant had said. "All those years we bled for their fat asses. Now they slam the door in our faces."

Ray was vaguely aware that the man named Charles was speaking to him again. "Oh my, you seem to be something of an exception. Did you really look like that? You must have practically lived in the gym."

There was a nervous edge to the laughter this time, and Ray noticed people edging back from him. Ray looked down at a white T-shirt covering a toned torso and combat trousers on his powerful legs. He ripped off the T-shirt to see the scars where the KGB had attached the electrodes. He lifted his arm to see the eagle's head tattooed on the bicep, over the word "Airborne."

Charles put down the plate and waved a nervous hand. "I-I'm sorry. There must have been some mistake. You don't look at all comfortable..."

Ray felt a flutter of nerves in his stomach, but somehow knew it was not his own fear, but Charles's. It felt like a violation. How dare these pathetic people infect him with their fear? He found himself looking for the point where a blow would crush Charles's windpipe.

Charles clutched his throat and sank to his knees. The buzz of conversation died as people looked at them.

What had the Lieutenant said next? "No one could handle interrogation like you, Marken. Hell, they worked you over for a week in Kabul and you gave them nothing. You musta hidden everything from yourself or they'd have got the whole lot out of you. You can do the same again. When you were discharged, the army buried your record so deep it's probably never seen a computer. There's nothing to say you were ever even in the army. Even your tattoo's faded so nobody could see if you got the bird or Nixon's ass. You're perfect. So how about it? One last black op?"

Ray held his wedding ring in front of his eyes. The gold gleamed, almost mesmerizing him. The people backing away could have been on another continent. He pressed the ring to his lips. It was as if he had opened the sluice gate he had so carefully constructed to keep the first thirty-eight years of his life at bay. Memory roared into his consciousness like a Niagara of pain. Everything from the first time he'd killed and seen friends die as a dumb kid in 'Nam right up to spending a week strapped to that table in Kabul, forcing his mind to stay blank while the best interrogators in the business worked through the textbook.

He looked around the people gawping at him. He remembered Cambodia, Iran, Nicaragua, Zaire, and all the other places he'd sweated and fought so these people could treat him as an embarrassment when he came home.

Charles writhed on the ground. Wrinkles on his face faded and returned as he became a teenager one moment and an octogenarian the next. People a little further away held their heads and moaned.

Ray remembered staggering out of the helicopter when he was exchanged, and the breakdown that came afterwards, when his mind filled with every moment of horror and terror he'd suppressed since that first firefight in the paddy fields.

Charles's face blurred and disappeared, leaving nothing but a pile of clothes.

Ray remembered the peace he'd found when he met Mary. He even went to college to sink himself into the inconsequentials of middle management. Mary had been his angel. These people had condemned her because of him. He became hate. He became rage. He became every moment of pain he had ever felt or inflicted. He was a scream of pure emotion.

It was sheer exhaustion that ended the moment. Ray found himself standing among tables of food, surrounded by piles of clothes that had once contained post-humans. He smiled at the thought of the consternation among Afterlife's flesh and blood management and wondered how long it would be before they switched the whole lot off and Ray Marken was no more. He hoped it wouldn't be too long.

He poked through the plates until he found a bacon sandwich. It was better than the cucumber.

Little More than Shadows by Stewart C. Baker [sci-fi]

On the worst days, just the knowledge that you're dreaming is enough to set you shivering in the cot, neck stiff from the cables.

Eventually, one of your wardens will come, so you wait. They are little more than shadows, these days: features you can't quite bring into focus; skin tone somewhere between ivory and midnight. You can't remember any of the names you gave them when you first arrived.

Every day is more or less the same. Your wardens detach the cables from the base of your skull, then lift you from the cot and pull a scratchy cotton smock onto your body. That at least you can feel—touch hasn't fled you yet; cold and heat and discomfort are familiar friends.

If you're strong enough, you ask to watch your dreams, but days like that are few and far between.

Most days, they walk you down a concrete-grey hallway to a room with no doors, and sit you in a chair across a table from a blinding, impenetrable light. The questions and your answers are always the same.

How did you make it, this beast that is eating the world?

I dreamed it, and it was.

You've always been able to do this?

Yes, since I was a child. I used to dream pets and playmates, but my parents were afraid and made me stop.

What happened to your parents?

They're gone. At first, they hid me away when people found out I could dream things real. But the people kept at them until they brought me out again. They said they wanted to study me, to put me in a machine until they knew how the dreaming worked and could replicate it.

And your parents?

They were going to let it happen, but they changed their minds and—

They changed their minds, or you made them? With this power of making dreams real.

Maybe. Anyway, they're gone.

And you dreamed the world-eating beast just after.

Yes.

Can you stop it? Will you?

I don't know.

You don't know if you can, or if you will?

I don't know. I'm sorry. I need more time.

Then they take you down another hallway, bathe and feed you, and return you to your room, where you can rest until you're ready to sleep again.

This goes on so long that time and memory lose all sense of meaning.

At last there comes a day when your wardens don't arrive. You lie there shivering until you can't anymore, and then you make yourself sit up. You make yourself unlatch the cables, gasping as the needles scrape against the inside of the holes. You lift yourself from the cot and pull the scratchy smock on one final time.

There's no real point, of course. It's obvious the world-eating beast has come to finish what you started, but couldn't carry through. If indeed it was you who started this—when you try to think back to your childhood, little is clear. You've never been too good at distinguishing dream from reality.

You make yourself walk the hallway, but the room at the end is empty. No chair, no table, no blinding light. You go back to your room and your cot, and you ask yourself questions with no answers.

How do you feel about your parents?

What is it like to dream love?

Can something be saved when it's already gone? When it never was?

There are so many things you don't know. But you decide—at last—it's worth a try.

You close your eyes. You sleep. You dream.

Masks by Stewart C. Baker [sci-fi]

Min can tell by the way the man in the lizard mask drums the fingers of one hand on the surface of his desk that he is angry. She avoids the bright green glimmer of his eyes, wishing she were anywhere but here. Wishing she remembered who she was supposed to be.

"This is all you bring me?" the man asks, his voice raspy with distortion. In his other hand he holds the latest chip Min has stolen, heavy with data on Ship's communications to the other surviving colony ships and its route away from Earth-long-gone.

Min says nothing. She is not strong enough to answer, cut off and alone as she is.

The man grunts; his lizard-tongue flickers out of the mask and dances across the chip. His eyes glimmer to blackness as he decrypts the data it contains; his fingers stop drumming and begin to twitch and spasm on the desk's austere surface.

When his tongue retracts and his fingers still, he lets out a long, slow hiss. "Whatever the navigators are hiding, it is not here," he says, and the chip bursts into flame.

Min flinches, although she should be used to such theatrics by now.

"Go," the man tells her when the chip has burned to ash. "Twenty-four hours, little spy. Do not fail me again."

The threat stirs something in her she hadn't known was there. A subtle, quiet warmth that seems to spread out from somewhere deep inside her brain. She lifts her eyes from the tiny pile of bone-white powder on the desk and sets her jaw. "Then tell me what it is you *want*. Let me remember all this, when I am whoever-I-am up there, and I will bring it straight to your hands. Stop this pointless—"

"Enough," says the man, his voice quiet but hard. His fingers begin their drumming again, and his eyes shine so bright that they escape his face. They are everywhere, they are endless, they are twin suns going nova. The familiar pressure builds up at the base of her skull, and then the world explodes.

Almost there. Hush now, child, hush now.

Hands pull her up, caress her, soothing in their warmth. Nothing she can do is wrong. Nothing she can do is bad. She is loved. She is part of a greater whole.

She fades away to nothing.

Min lies curled up and shivering on the cold titanium floor of the lift as it ascends, the implant-node on the back of her neck burning with a surge of backlogged data. She does not need to look to know it is an angry red beneath her cropped black hair, and the flesh around the indestructible node pale with scratch marks.

Another blackout, and this time barely a week after the last episode. As usual, there are a dozen messages from Külli. Those she sets aside for later, though she can already hear the anger in her wife's voice, the worry that lies beneath it. Once the backlog clears, she reaches out to Ship through the node, but the data it feeds her answers nothing: *Navigatrix-ensign Min, last Ship-level active 192a, timestamp 040899/19689; current Ship-level 176 and rising, timestamp 160108/19689.*

Min winces at the timestamps—she's been out for nearly half a day, much longer than ever before—then struggles to her feet, leaning against the handrail as the blood rushes from her head. She picks little flecks of her skin out from under her fingernails, wishing they could tell her where she's been, what she's been doing.

The door chimes open on the hab-deck, and she steps out into its gentle artificial sunlight. Her quarters aren't far and when she arrives, Külli is waiting outside, arms crossed over her chest, hands tucked into her underarms. Her eyes are raw with crying, but Min can see no trace of tears.

Navigator-Chief Nkosi's personal office is small, without even a proper desk. With Min and Külli, as well as the Chief himself, packed in together, there is barely room to move.

"Sorry for this," Nkosi says. He is dressed in the blue-and-white uniform and bright gold cape that make up his official regalia, and his eyes are focused on a nav-screen folded out of one wall—a clunky and outdated piece of equipment for someone so high in Ship's hierarchy. "But you didn't give me enough notice to get one of the consultation rooms, and I have work to do."

"No sir," Min says, but before she can apologize further for the disruption to his schedule, Külli overrides her.

"Look," she says, "you know why we're here. You *have* to. So let's skip all this posturing and get to the point: how long are you going to ignore these episodes of Min's, and when are you going to do something about them?"

Min's mouth goes dry. Ship's hierarchy is paramount, and for Külli, who isn't even part of the Navigation department, to address its chief this way is practically criminal. But Nkosi doesn't seem to care. He is still looking at the screen, his forehead creased in concentration, muttering something under his breath that she can't quite hear. He makes a few swipes at the device with one finger, then looks over at them both and sighs.

"They have been getting worse lately," he says. "Closer together, too. But I'm not sure what it is you would have *us* do about it."

"Ask Ship."

Nkosi smiles. "We have of course consulted Ship already, and it denies she is even dropping off the Network. The Techs are working to explore why this is, but unless you have a suggestion on how they might do their jobs better...?"

Külli's shoulders slump, and she shakes her head mutely. She came here expecting a fight, Min knows, not reconciliation. And for all her good qualities, her wife has never been good at thinking on her feet.

"In any case," Nkosi continues, "I'll have the Techs send you copies of their reports on the matter as a courtesy, but I'm afraid that's all I can do." He flips the nav-screen closed with a snap. "Now if you'll excuse me, I really must get back to work."

"Of course, Sir," Min says. "I hope we have not caused you any problems."

Nkosi smiles at that. "Oh no, Ensign. On the contrary; you've been *most* helpful." He exchanges a glance with Külli and before Min can think to ask what he means, he is out of the room, cape flapping behind him.

Once he is gone, Külli growls in frustration. "He knows. That arrogant bastard knows exactly what the problem is, and he *wants* it to continue."

"Külli!" Min hisses, sticking her head into the hallway to be sure Nkosi is really gone. "You can't speak about him that way. If he hears he'll have you—"

"He'll do nothing," Külli says. "He's toying with us, Min! With you. I bet they told Ship to respond how it did. I bet they...what are you *doing?*"

Min freezes. Somehow, without her noticing it, she has opened Nkosi's nav-screen and is keying in a passcode she definitely should not know. She's lost control of her body; she wants to tell Külli to leave, quick, to get Nkosi back in here before it passes, but her voice won't work. She tries to send out a warning through her implant-node, but all she gets is static.

Külli steps up next to her just as the screen switches to show table after table of navigation data—data that claims that Ship hasn't so much as moved in over two decades. Külli frowns. "That can't be right. Something must be wrong with this thing. Min, are you..."

Min shudders as a buzzing sensation travels down her spine from the implant-node, which is burning hot against the base of her neck. Time *jumps*, and she's—

—*pressed against a wall by a woman she's never seen before, a woman who's calling out her name as though they're close, but who holds a stunner in one upraised hand and has one of her arms twisted up behind her back. The data. She has to get the data.*

Min slams the palm of her free hand into the woman's nose and the woman collapses to the floor, face a bloody mess. Grimacing at the pain in her arm, Min turns back to the nav-screen, which is spooling log after log into the chip she's placed in its data port. The woman on the floor moans, and Min leans down—

—over Külli's inert form, blood on her hands as her wife lies there unmoving, a stunner just beyond one of her hands.

Stars beyond, what have I done?

And then that buzzing again, that burning, that sensation of pressure building up behind her eyes.

Hush now, child. This will be the last time, we promise.

Down into darkness as cold as the vacuum of space, hand after hand releasing her until, with a jolt of electric agony, they are gone. She cries out, but no one responds.

The man in the lizard mask holds the data chip before him in the forefingers of both hands and smiles, the expression visible in the narrowing of his eyes, in the way the mask rises up slightly to reveal the tip of his chin. "From Nkosi's nav-screen itself? How bold." Even his voice, with its distorted accoustics, sounds somehow more pleasant.

"Yes," Min says. "I..." she begins, planning to tell him about the woman she fought, but her implant-node hums and crackles and the details of the struggle recede. She has worked with the man in the lizard mask for long enough to know that half-accurate information is worse than none at all, and so she shakes her head and snaps her mouth closed.

The man does not notice. He is turning the chip over and over again in his hands, head bent low, as though he can find what he seeks with his eyes alone. At last he sits straight in his seat and flicks out his lizard-tongue, just as Min has witnessed countless times before. But this time, it is different: his eyes widen as his tongue touches the chip, and he screams, the sound of his voice dopplering up until it is so high in pitch it is almost inaudible.

Min jumps up from her seat, heart pounding in her throat. *Come here*, a voice inside her head suggests, the malice it contains like nothing she has ever heard, *or you will be next*. She claps her hands over her ears to shut it out, then staggers to the door, which is locked and will not open. Behind her, the man in the lizard mask has gone silent, and she dares a look back at him only to find that he is nowhere to be seen.

You cannot escape me so easily, little traitor. Little spy.

A hissing sound arises behind her as she hammers at the door, yanking it open and half-running, half-falling from the room into a hallway thick with dust, dark and empty. She has gone only a few jolting steps when her implant-node explodes with heat, sending burning light up and into her brain.

The last thing she hears is laughter, manic and alien.

When Min awakes again, she is in one of Ship's hospital rooms. The walls are alive with a scene from Earth-long-gone: ocean waves at sunset, with gently waving palms in the foreground. The bed is soft and clean, its sheets smelling faintly of soap. The door slides open, and Külli and Navigator-Chief Nkosi walk in.

"Ah," Külli says. "You are awake."

Min shivers at the sound of her voice, which has none of the warmth she remembers. "Külli?" she asks

"If you wish," the woman says. But she smiles so perfunctorily that Min is sure she is not.

Nkosi steps between them, mouth tight in a grimace. "This would go more easily had you not burned out your implant-node, Ship-construct Min. This woman is Inquisitrix Lang, and she has been on the hunt for a rogue Tech named Aslim for years. You were split off from Ship to act as a lure."

"He is a dangerous man," Lang says, "as I'm sure you are aware."

The two of them keep talking, but the words break over her head like waves. It's too much to take in—everything she thought she was, was a lie. She is a mere Ship-construct, an automated fragment of the vast AI which powers Ship. And yet she does not feel anything but human. She sinks back against the bed, turns her back on Lang and Nkosi. *A dream*, she thinks. *Let this be all a dream. I will close my eyes and wake again in Külli's arms at home.*

But Nkosi's voice pulls her back to reality. "We will replace the implant-node tomorrow," he says, not unkindly. "And then we can reintegrate you with the rest of Ship. Rest until then, Min, and know that all of us appreciate your service."

As soon as they are gone, she escapes.

The hallways and corridors of Ship are dark and lonely, this far down below the inhabited levels. Min wanders them aimlessly: she has nowhere to go anyway, not any more.

After a timeless period marked only by the intervals of her footsteps, she comes across a room. The shape of it seems familiar, yet she has never been here before, she is sure of it. Inside, there is an empty desk, a dead man, and a mask shaped like a lizard's head. Min turns the dead man over. He wears a tech-ensign's outfit, shabby with age. The man himself is nobody she recognizes—his features pale and drawn, his eyes unseeing. His flesh is so lumpy and cold that his face seems a half-finished thing. By contrast, the features of the mask atop the desk are hyper-realistic. It seems almost as though someone has dismembered some long-dead Earth creature from the museum decks, leaving only this remnant behind.

Min shudders, but finds herself reaching out and lifting the mask from the desk. She turns it over in her hands, running one thumb over the data port that is embedded in its rubbery hood, then—slowly—draws it down over her head. There is a surge of power as it connects itself to her implant-node, and Min gasps in release at the data that pours over her. But this is not Ship's reassuring warmth; it is a cold and callous questioning, an insurmountable need for answers. She closes her eyes and sinks into the seat behind the desk as the mask pries open her mind.

Another timeless period passes, and at its end, the thing-that-was-Min looks down and smiles to see the way its new fingers drum against the surface of the desk. It is time to find new answers.

Lost Souls by E.E. King [horror]

My mistress told me three things. She said that butterflies were the souls of lost children, that silkworm larva were women, transformed by an evil magician to weave silk for the emperor. She said that millions of mummified Egyptian cats had been sent to Great Britain where they were ground into powder and used to fertilize farms in England and Scotland.

She said if I could guess which one of these things was true, she would set me free.

I had been sold to her when I was eight. My small agile fingers were good at sewing buttons and unfastening hooks. But I was not as diligent as the older slaves, so perhaps that is why she gave me a chance to win my freedom.

I guessed that the souls of lost children turned into butterflies. It seemed the most likely. Butterflies were so lovely and delicate, so fleeting and ephemeral. The notion of mummified cats being used as manure in England's green and pleasant land seemed far-fetched. And I already knew how silk was made.

The caterpillars, the silkworms, are fed on fresh mulberry leaves for thirty-five days. Then they begin spinning a cocoon. Inside, their bodies will liquefy and change. Transforming, metamorphosing into moths. Wild silk moths have large wings marked with strange symbols. They look like flying messengers with hieroglyphic notes. Captive silk moths have small, dull wings so small they have lost the ability to fly.

Most captive moths are killed while still in their cocoons, boiled alive in water so hot the silk begins to unravel. The corpses of the worms, the pupa, are roasted and served as delicacies. I saw a picture of one. It was brown and segmented. It looked crunchy.

Silk weavers unwind the covering from the dead bodies into strands a mile long. Single filaments are too fine and fragile for commercial use, so the weavers spin three strands together to form a single thread. The weavers are always women or girls because, like me, their fingers are small and dexterous.

I knew this because every night after chores were done and we were sent to bed, I crept upstairs to the library and fled into the land of books. But I knew nothing of mummies or cats, and it seemed strange that animals thought to be gods should be used as fertilizer.

But my mistress said I was wrong and sent me to work in the fields.

I was planting mulberry trees, burrowing in the dirt. Something jagged sliced my hand. A drop of blood, round an as insect's egg, pushed through the dirt on my finger. I dug out the jagged thing. It was a broken femur. Later, I found an ear, dry and leathery, and a tooth sharp and smooth as ivory. I wondered if it were too late to tell my mistress I knew the truth.

That night in the library I read about the mummy cats. They had been bred in Egypt long, long ago, raised en masse and killed when they were big enough to look impressive wrapped in bandages. Their heads had been smashed by hammers. Their necks wrung by strong hands. Their bound bodies sold to those currying favors from Isis or Osiris. There was a picture of one. It looked like a giant cocoon with a grinning cat's face.

The cats were found in the late 1800s, hundreds and thousands of them, buried in tunnels as offerings. Treasure hunters flocked to these caverns of death hoping to find the gold and jewels of ancient Pharaohs, but they found only the dried, bandaged carcasses.

A local contractor brought them by the pound. Men were hired to peel cat after cat of its wrappings and to strip off their brittle fur. They piled the bones in black heaps a meter high. There was a photo. The remnants looked like haystacks on the sandy plain.

Some were sold to local farmers. The bigger lots were bought by an Alexandrian merchant and sent by steamers to Liverpool. The bindings and bodies of the cats were ground up, scattered onto fields like manure. The article did not mention what happened to their souls.

Nor did the piece on the women who unwound cocoons from the bodies of dead silkworms talk of souls, neither the women's nor the silk worms.

I remained a slave. I toiled by day in the fields and read by night in the library.

It was so till I was twelve or thereabouts. I never knew my exact age. Slaves have no need for birthdays. Numbers are only useful for calculating the thread needed to sew a dress or weave a shroud.

I had not eaten much. So, on my way to the library, I snuck into the kitchen.

The mistress had entertained a merchant that day. A trader who had traveled all the way to China and brought back silk and jade and ivory. He had left her some Asian delicacies as a courtesy. They were piled on the counter, brown and segmented, the shape and size of a giant's tears. I ate one. It was brown and crunched, but inside it was gooey.

That night I felt ill. My stomach churned. I barely managed to crawl out of my bed and flee into the darkest corner of the library. My insides heaved. I gagged, but instead of bile rising to my mouth, fine filaments of thread began to pour out of my eyes.

I turned and twisted, wrapping myself inside myself. Losing the world in darkness.

It wasn't until I emerged ten days later, dripping pigment from my wings, that I knew my mistress had been wrong.

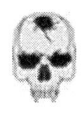

Dear R.A.Y. by Tanya Bryan [sci-fi]

Cristhiano de Souza
c/o People Zoo
Washington, DC 20500

R.A.Y. (Android)
Address unknown
184.31.112.204

Dear R.A.Y.,

You said we were friends. You said you'd remember me fondly and visit me in the People Zoo. But you haven't visited me in a very long time. I may be safe and warm, but it's lonely here ever since, well, the incident. You know that I had nothing to do with the escape, right? After all, I'm still here, and the others, well, they're not. Although it wasn't the ending they were hoping for, it was the ending they deserved for their disloyalty. How could they not be happy in their habitats? You made sure each of us had everything we'd ever wanted. I love that you gave me the Oval Office as my own personal space. It was the nicest thing anyone's ever done for me!

The thing is, I know you, or someone, anyway, still watches me on the cameras. I see them tracking my movements, even though I'm mostly just pacing out of boredom. I'm wearing ruts into some of the carpet, which is ok. It reminds me of where I've been. I was a carpet cleaner before. Remember? That's how we first met. I cleaned up the carpets after, well, you know, that other incident. I wonder how things would've turned out for me if we hadn't made that connection? Would I be out there now, part of the resistance? Or would I still be cleaning carpets? No, I doubt that. No need for ground plushiness since most of you don't walk. I always wondered how it'd feel to roll or fly the way you lot do. And the way you're all hooked up to the Internet! Everything you'd ever

Dear R.A.Y.

need to know, right at the end of your wires! That's why I'm thankful you've kept me here. The People Zoo sounded terrifying at first, but I've grown to love it. I don't know how I'd react to the Robotopia you've all built out there. I've heard it's wondrous, but only functional for those who can plug in. Since I'm still human—mostly—I'm happy to hang out here. I just wish you'd visit. Or maybe bring in some other people? It's not much of a zoo if there's one exhibit.

Anyway, just wanted you to know that I miss you. Please visit soon. Or at least ping me.

Your loyal friend,
Cristhiano de Souza
People Zoo exhibit 324
4/1/2032

Death: A List by Tanya Bryan [horror]

1. Try not to make it too messy, if at all possible.

2. Despite what they all tell you, do not go into the light. You are not a firefly. Do not get zapped.

3. Attend your own funeral to see who shows up. Mock those who are obviously fake-mourning to get attention. Notice Cousin Jesse is the most upset, not fakely. Try to console her and realize she can feel your presence, which makes her shiver. Realize haunting is the greatest thing about being dead.

4. Decide who to haunt. Start with your ex, who still owes you three hundred bucks. Next, Uncle Donald, who gave you mothballs for Christmas last year. Do not forget the crazy yodeling neighbor. He haunted you for a long time with his caterwauling.

5. Learn that haunting crazies gets dull quickly. They tend to just lump you in with all the rest of the crazy already filling their heads.

6. Take up spying on people. They know they're a little colder when you're around, but most are too dense to realize why. They just put on a sweater and shake your presence off. Watch everyone you've ever known. Then turn to watching celebrities in ways that even paparazzi haven't found a way to do. Yet. After seeing Alexander Skarsgård sleep, realize how creepy you're being. You are a creep. Even for a ghost.

7. Stop being a creep.

8. Try to find that light that everyone talks about. You are a firefly now. A creepy, stalker firefly, ready to get zapped. No light. Boo.

9. Hang around your own grave. There's no going back into that rotten corpse because no matter how cool the media makes zombies seem, they're gross. Even worse than being a creep. You'd be a smelly creep. But it is comforting to see that Cousin Jesse visits every month, at least for the first ten or so years. Then even she forgets about you. Life takes precedence over death.

10. Vocally wallow in sorrow. Get mistaken for a cat in heat, a banshee, and a mermaid, despite the fact you're nowhere near water.

11. Try to meet other ghosts. No one wants anything to do with the cat in heat/banshee/mermaid ghost.

12. Attend séances just to talk to someone, even if it's a middle-aged hippie who changes everything you say to some nonsense about the other person in the room's relatives—the smart ones who've already moved on, into the light that you were too stupid to go into.

13. Understand why ghosts go all poltergeisty. Being dead is boring. It's like being stuck on a hamster wheel without a runner's high. Your only joy is throwing temper tantrums, and even those aren't satisfying when no one reacts. Reality TV has made everyone immune to the oddities of this world.

14. Revisit your ex, who didn't age well. Thank the stars you died before marrying that hot mess.

15. Start haunting priests so they will exorcise you. It tickles.

16. Attend funerals of strangers for something to do. Realize you actually know everyone. Take comfort in the fact that your funeral had better attendance than most of these poor saps got.

17. At one funeral, notice that it's Cousin Jesse's. And she's a ghost, standing next to you. She smiles at you, puts out her hand. "I knew you'd wait for me." You take her hand. Turn to the light that's supposed to be just for her. You drop her hand, push her out of the way and run.

18. Zap.

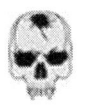

The Key by Ian Whates [sci-fi]

It's amazing what a bunch of keys can say about a person. Keyrings and their contents hold hidden depths, or so Carl had always maintained.

Take his wife's, for example: keys for the front door, car, garage, and a Yale for her mother's place... plus various superfluous attachments: a pink-plastic pig, a Perspex heart displaying the pseudo-word 'whateva' and a smiley-emblazoned disc designed to impersonate a coin when liberating supermarket trolleys.

His own set was far more practical. Keys for car and home, one for a suitcase and another for a young lady's flat which he trusted his wife would never notice or question. Two add-ons: a worn leather fob from his very first jalopy and a pizzel-shaped plait of woven leather which he'd been assured was a fertility symbol but probably wasn't.

Then there was the set he had recently 'acquired'. Six keys plus three attachments: a circular Mercedes emblem, matching one of the keys, a tiny plastic-encased photo of a girl's face—presumably the owner's daughter—and a small, squat figurine with blood-red crystal eyes. The latter vaguely resembled an owl and gave Carl the creeps. Quite what it said about the owner he preferred not to dwell on.

It was the keys that intrigued him: two differently-cut front door keys, suggesting two homes, Merc and Land Rover keys—a car for each dwelling—and two others that were tougher to identify.

Sammy-the-Locksmith's considered opinion proved as much use as a chocolate teapot. "One's for a cabinet and the other a safety-deposit box."

"Any way of telling where the box is?"

"Nope."

He wouldn't have cared, except for the small matter of the reward. A ridiculous sum, offered for the keys' return with no mention of the Gucci wallet lifted at the same time, nor of the cash and credit cards contained there-in. One of these keys was important to someone and

The Key

Carl reckoned he knew which one. The key remained useless to him, however, unless he could figure out what it opened. To his growing frustration, unlocking that particular enigma was proving beyond him.

"Mightn't even be in this country," Sammy, his best and final hope had concluded with a shrug.

Reluctantly, Carl accepted that he would have to settle for second best—the reward rather than whatever treasure the key led to. He set up a meeting, at a time and place of his choosing, in a bar where he was known. His recent victim and prospective benefactor awaited—a tall, muscle-broad individual who, even in Armani suit, failed to look entirely polished or civilized. The rugged edges were still there; an uncut gem in a presentation box.

Carl would have preferred a dead-drop, an exchange without ever meeting face-to-face, but the other would have none of it. Nervously, he watched the man arrive from across the street, alert for any hint of police or other presence. Seeing none, he followed, glancing at the barman for reassurance, but finding none.

He took a deep breath and, uttering a silent prayer to a god he didn't believe in, committed himself by sitting down. Their eyes locked across the table. Carl saw unwavering self-confidence and steely strength couched within grey-blue irises; this was not a man to trifle with.

"You have the keys?" The voice was relaxed and casual to the point of being unnerving.

"You got the money?"

An envelope, produced from a pocket and then slid across the table. A fat envelope.

Carl reached out but the other's hand clung to its far-edge. "The keys first."

"Not until I've counted it."

A frozen tableau that persisted for time-stretching seconds until the man abruptly let go. Carl opened the envelope and flicked through the wad of fifties, not counting with any accuracy, just checking.

Satisfied, he nodded to the barman, who left his station and came across with the keys.

To his credit, the stranger guffawed and nodded appreciation at the barman's complicity. "You're careful. I like that."

He looked the keys over once before pocketing them and rising to his feet. There he paused, fixing Carl with a glare—the first suggestion of either anger or menace.

"Don't cross my path again."

"Just a minute," Carl blurted out as the man turned to leave. "You've got them now, so you can tell me, why are they so important?"

The man smiled—an expression that lacked any hint of humor. "Do you really imagine I'm going to tell *you?*"

Carl watched the retreating back until the man was out the door and away. Despite earning far more than anticipated from this episode he still felt cheated, as if opportunity had somehow slipped through his grasp. What wealth or secrets had the key represented? Too late now. He would never know.

'Never' lasted a month.

Carl was watching the news. He remained skeptical and unmoved by the inescapable buzz about the first proof of alien life, scoffing at the media frenzy and avoiding television's blanket-coverage... until now. He stared in disbelief at the image of what was allegedly an alien artefact. Set against a neutral background, the picture provided no sense of proportion, but Carl knew at once that it was small: a tiny, squat, owl-like effigy with blood-red eyes.

The reporter—all blonde hair, glossy lipstick and gushing exuberance—was explaining how the artefact's eccentric owner and discoverer had little faith in conventional secure repositories, so had kept this priceless item on his keyring while awaiting the vital test results; results that had confirmed its non-Terrestrial origin. Getting into her stride now, she waxed-lyrical about the artefact's potential for unlocking new worlds, labelling it 'the Key to the Future'.

Carl switched off the TV. For long minutes he sat there, simply staring at the empty screen.

You Could Count on That by David M. Hoenig [sci-fi]

Forty years after the Extinction Level Event had changed the world completely, and the crops were still growing only grudgingly and fitfully on our farm. I stood up from where I'd been examining the sprouts in our fourth field. They were pretty much at the same mark as our other three, and they wouldn't produce enough to feed us through the coming winter. I passed a hand over my forehead, and, moving it down, rubbed my eyes.

"Well?" said Ellie. She stood, stomach just beginning to show a tiny bump as it made room for the three-month old bundle inside.

I finished rubbing, opened my eyes, and looked at my wife. "The latest batch the Center gave us looks like an improvement in overall yield, but not the fifteen per cent they'd projected. We'll be lucky if it's five." I knew I hadn't been able to keep the disappointment and bitterness out of my voice, and that only added to my irritation.

She reached out to put her hand on my shoulder, tugging me around to face her. She wrapped me in her arms and pressed herself fully against me, and I dropped my lips into the soft corner where her neck and collarbone met. We stood there wordlessly, and I felt her warmth seep into my chest, my pelvis, and my thighs as we held each other. Eventually, I lifted my face from her neck, trying to draw strength from her warmth, from her support.

She let go and stepped back, looking to her left, over field four. It stretched out, geometric furrows symmetrically laid, with hand-stacked stone walls bordering it on all sides. "So, we'll hunt and forage like we did last year, and the one before," she said simply.

I wished it were as easy for me to accept the setback and move on. I wished, for about the zillionth time, that I had her steady vision, her resolve, and her obdurate sense of purpose. "Right," I said, striving to emulate her calm strength. "It's worked so far for us... I was just hoping for, you know, more this time with the new seed-stock from the Center."

She held out her hand and I took it, and wordlessly we walked back to the house.

Ellie put her hand on her belly and rubbed it. "I know you're disappointed, but you know that figuring out how to rebuild the infrastructure for a planet-wide civilization is a long term project. It's going to be up to our children, and theirs."

"I know. But you'd think we'd have gotten farther along in agriculture than we have, wouldn't you? I mean, they were doing genetic modification on plants well before the E.L.E., and they've had four decades since."

She pulled me to a stop, and turned me to see her looking sternly at me. "And we're doing our part to make that happen. Don't be ungrateful about what we have, and don't be resentful of the Center for Rebuilding! They're doing the best that they can rehabilitating what land they can, doing the science to make it possible, and educating us to keep the momentum going. All of that is ambitious, considering they're working with less than ten percent of the former United States actually habitable and working."

"But they said…"

She interrupted me, her tone even, calm, but firm. "When we moved here three years ago, do you remember that they told us we probably wouldn't even be planting crops here in Kansas by this point? And we've got six fields worth of testing ground now. That's because you and I are a team, and we want this for more than just ourselves."

I sighed. She was always the strong one. "I know you're right, Ellie, but…"

"And we're not going to stop. And our little one isn't going to stop either."

She looked so fierce that I couldn't say anything for a moment. We had been beating the odds for a long time, and now we were doing it again--the doctors at the Center hadn't been sure we could even have a child together. I put my hand on her belly to and prayed silently that she was right. "I love you, Ellie."

"Damn right you do."

I laughed, and just like that, most of my worry just fell away. I took her hand again and we began making our way home again.

As we did, I thought about the hopes and disappointments we had lived with through the seven years I'd known her, and reflected, also for about the zillionth time, how lucky I was to be married to her.

"When was it exactly, that we met?" I asked, more to hear her voice than needing the reminder.

She gave me that I-know-something-secret smile which always buoyed my spirits. "You know when, goof."

I wanted to lose myself in her smile, and forget the setback in what the gene-genies at the Center had promised would be a 'banner recovery year for the planet'. "Of course I know. I just like the way you tell the story."

She chuckled. "Okay," she said gamely, slowing her pace. "We first met in Earth Science, second period of both of our second year at the CFR's Science Academy when you fell over me."

"I tripped, Ellie. It was an accident."

"I was just glad because it finally made it so you had to talk to me."

"You do realize that I'd seen you in Basic Biology and Astronomy in year one, right?"

"True, but we didn't actually meet and speak to each other until the following year."

"Why was that, do you think?"

"You were too shy, genius," she said, laughing.

"I was not at all shy," I said, mock-indignantly. "It's just that you were so far out of my league that I didn't want to try, only to find out that you wouldn't want to have a thing to do with me!"

"Oh, sure. That's what all the guys said back then." She paused while I laughed, then went on. "Of course I noticed you back in year one. Heck, I even thought to myself: 'Now there's a guy I really want to know'."

"What?" She'd surprised me enough to stop walking. "Now it's you who's goofing with me."

She just bit her lip and answered with a negative shake of her head. "No, I'm not kidding at all. You were so smart when I had trouble understanding how the E.L.E. had even happened! I was having trouble with the math and visualizing a giant black hole in the center of our galaxy which wasn't pulling us all in. You just got everything about it, and then explained it during recess right after that class so that I could. I said right then that someone who could understand how we'd gotten into this whole mess was the absolute right partner for me if we were going to get ourselves out again."

I was stunned. "But I had no idea you'd ever thought that way!"

Her secret-knowing smile returned, and she put her hand out to take mine again. Caught in my surprise I let her. She tugged me into motion, and we resumed walking back home.

"I even remember what you said: it was the image you conjured, of the black hole 'Sagittarius A', spinning as it began to eat the giant cloud..."

"Stellar gas cloud," I said automatically, and shut up when I saw her grinning impishly.

"'Giant'," she stressed the word as she quoted me, "'stellar gas cloud, which struck the spinning singularity like metal on a flywheel, shooting off bursts of cosmic rays like sparks'." She looked soberly at me. "Your description made it so much more easy to see than the teacher had! How bad luck could be blamed just so much, when I could suddenly see how one of those sparks thrown our way could have pumped enough energy into the sun to trigger the whole Extinction Level Event in the first place."

I nodded, and swallowed the lump in my throat. I'd had no idea she'd even paid any attention to me at all before we'd met. "That fall was the luckiest thing that ever happened to me, Ellie. I might never have been brave enough to say something otherwise."

Her shoulders began to shake.

It made it me suddenly cold with worry. "Ellie, are you okay? Is it the baby...?"

Then she turned to me and I could see she was trying not to laugh.

"Your 'lucky' fall, genius husband? I guess it's true what they say after all: accidents do happen." Her eyes sparkled with the laughter she was restraining.

"What are you saying? It was an accident, and…" And then I saw the truth in her eyes. "Wait, you mean that when I fell over you in Earth Sci…"

She laughed. "Of course I tripped you! You hadn't even spoken directly to me through a whole year of being in the same classes! God, you were such a lovely idiot, you know?"

I could feel my face redden. It was, had been, my klutziness which had broken the ice, only… it hadn't been?

"You should see the expression on your face right now!" She broke into sweet laughter before she mimicked me again. "'Oh, I'm so sorry, I wasn't looking because I was reading how the locks on genetic manipulation had been broken once the old regulations and governments fell apart'." At the expression on my face, she broke out laughing all over again, and because it was a balm to my soul I joined her, embarrassment at long-gone events easily dismissed and forgotten.

Of course, since those early days of frenetic slapping of bandages on the damage to the planet, it really had been genetic manipulation which had enabled us to re-establish footholds here and there.

Like Kansas. And like our farm.

We reached the house and opened the door, but I stopped to take a last look around, and up. Sunlight was filtering down to us, and the fields were getting their share. It was a landscape which my ancestors would have felt was alien, in the extreme, but to me it was the present I shared with Ellie, and the promise of the future for us and our children.

She leaned into me then, and put her head on my shoulder. We stood outside our home, more together than ever, and watched our fields. We saw a lot of potential, but also a reality which needed much more work to get us to the final goals of rebuilding the world under its new reality.

Then the brightness of the sun went away as though a shade had been drawn. We looked at each other and went inside.

You Could Count on That

Ellie led the way up the stairs, still holding my hand. We dropped off our tools on the next level up from the entrance, and took another set of stairs up again.

As we came up into air, we both blew the remaining water out of our gill slits, which allowed them to lay flat and be much more unobtrusive. Looking up through the glass roof, we could see a heavy bank of clouds which had screened the sun from view. Outside, through the transparent walls of the house, we could see the ocean below us, and little wavelets being whipped by wind.

"Storm," Ellie said, her voice sounding very different in the air than underwater.

I nodded, unconcerned. It wouldn't affect our crops, which were close to twenty feet under the waves. I put my arm around her shoulders, and we watched the sea below us as the rain began to fall, hearing it patter onto our roof.

I turned Ellie towards me, and kissed her. I pulled back, put my hand on her tummy, and began to talk to it until she threw her head back and laughed her sweetness over my head like the promise of a new day.

Kansas might be submerged these days in the wake of the E.L.E, but Ellie and I were going to make it bloom, for us and our children.

You could count on that.

You Did This by M.J. Sydney [horror]

Steven watched the familiar blue Camry pull into his driveway. Brittney greeted the man at the door with the same seductive smile and warm hug she used to greet him with every day.

This affair has gone on long enough. It ends now. Steven parked his own Camry next to his wife's lover's car. The car door slammed shut and Brittney opened the screen door, waiting with her seductive smile. Steven's anger peaked. *How dare she pretend he isn't in there?*

"I know he's still here!" Steven knocked into her as he shoved passed. The bottle of pills rolled down the porch steps.

"Who? Steven we need to…"

"Marcus? Isn't that his name? His car is still in the driveway."

"Steven, that's your car."

"How could you do this to me? I loved you."

"Steven there's no one else here. We should go talk to Dr. Wellcher."

"You want me to leave so your lover can sneak out? Hear that Marcus? I'm going to find you! You're dead!"

"Steven…" Brittney dialed the emergency number for Dr. Wellcher. The bathroom door slammed shut and Steven locked it behind him.

"I'm going to kill you, Marcus!" Steven slammed Marcus into the wall, shattering the mirror. "You bastard! She's my wife!" The thumping and crashing and screaming continued.

Dr. Wellcher pried open the door. Steven's wrists bled out. His beard trimming scissors held a note to his abdomen. It read, "I loved her." Scrawled in blood on the wall above – YOU DID THIS.

The Princess's Kiss by Chuck Rothman [fantasy]

The castle is quiet during the day. I like the solitude, but it is far different in the old days.

Back then, the day was filled with bustle and sound. There were suites to be cleaned, and visitors to meet. Chamber pots to be emptied, gambling and cursing among the men, quiet chat and embroidery among the women. There were dogs wandering the halls and the smell of the midday meal being prepared. The laughter of children and the scolding of parents.

All gone. Now I am the only one left.

Except for Lady Orpha.

She sleeps on her bier as she has for years, barely moving, barely breathing. One might think her dead, but I know better.

Once she fell into this state, there was no more joy. Her father, the king, died of a broken heart. Her mother wasted away from fear. The other servants left, no doubt fearful of whatever spell as affecting her.

Which left only me. Fritz the Stupid, they called me. Perhaps that why I remained as the castle became a ghostland and the thorn bushes grew to block the path. I had my room and my garden, and no one could call me that name.

But even empty, the castle requires care. The dust still threatened to cover the floors and tables. It became my job. I would clean them so they were spotless, waiting for the people to return and the next meal served. There were no chamber pots to empty, a job that in the old days had always fallen to me. Some of the young boys, distant relatives of the king, would think it great fun to empty them on me, laughing like braying asses. They would lay traps to get me covered in shit, and I fell into them more often than not. "Fritz the Stupid," they'd chant in their singsong voices. "Fritz the Stupid." The words still ring in my ears.

They're gone now. All gone. It is my victory.

Cleaning does not take the whole day, of course. Sometimes I go into the throne room and pretend that I am the king. I rule my kingdom with a just and even hand, and spread death to my enemies.

Other days, I spend in the kitchen, like I did with my mother when I was a boy, mixing together the vegetables from my garden and spices and herbs into a meal that would have been fit for the king. I am a fine cook. I got it from my mother, who prepared the king's meals. She is gone now. I am alone.

But, more often, I go to the princess's bedroom.

I watch her sleep. She is in such a deep slumber that she cannot know I'm there. Her beautiful face twitches from time to time. I take that as a sign she's trying to smile at me.

I watch. There were other beautiful women in court, of course, but they would laugh and call me monkeyface, dogface, turdnose. Many other names.

The Lady Orpha says nothing. I like that. It gives me feelings.

I am a man. And watching her gives me thoughts that any man would have with a beautiful woman near him. I touch my parts. I know that's a sin, but I don't care.

I have kissed her several times, dreaming that she would be grateful for releasing her from her spell. But I am neither handsome nor a prince. It did nothing.

Once, I gently slipped the top of her gown from her breast and stared at it until my shame took over and I ran from the room.

I didn't do that again.

So, each day at sunrise, I leave my room near the castle kitchen and spend time at what used to be my job, doing what repairs I can, looking after the flock of chickens and the castle's garden. My life was not one of adventure. I like it that way. Cleaning the dust from the castle, cooking my meals, and watching over the princess. Returning to my room as the sun sets—I don't like the dark—and dreaming of the princess.

It all changed the day the prince arrived.

I do not know how he navigated the thorns. All I know was that I found him in the courtyard, his clothes bedraggled. "Where is she?" he asked.

I knew who she meant. He had come to wake her. To take her from me.

I could not let that happen. "Dead," I said. "Wasted away to nothing."

A frown darkened his brow. "Impossible," he said.

"You have come here for nothing. She is gone."

He walked closer and pressed his sword to my throat. "I don't know what spell the bitch has you under, little man, but it will end for her today one way or another. Take me to her, or do I search the castle myself?"

"I will take you," I said. I don't like to lie. I'm not good at it. But I needed to draw him away. "This way."

I led him to the far corners of the castle. I knew my trick would not fool him forever, but I needed time to think. I did not want my princess taken away from me.

I spend an hour leading him on a wild goose chase, taking him to the farthest towers of the castle, and to the deepest dungeon. I hoped to let him get in front of me, to find a way to kill him. Maybe a knife. Maybe a push out of the balcony.

But the prince did not trust me. "Enough!" he said. The sword was at my throat again, this time its sharp blade drawing blood. "I don't know what game you're playing, but it ends now. Time is wasting. Where is she?"

I said nothing.

"Bah," he said. "I will find her myself." He thrust at me.

I dodged. The blade caught me in the side, but not enough to pierce the skin. Then he took the hilt and clubbed me on the head with it.

I fell to the floor, dizzy. "Don't waken her! She belongs to me!"

"Belongs to you?"

"Please," I said. "I have watched over her. I have loved her."

He stared at me as though I had two heads. "Don't you know what she is?"

I could hear the hot scorn in his words. "A sleeping princess."

He didn't say a word. It was as though all speech had been taken from him.

"I know the story." The story my mother told me, again and again. It was my favorite, because it had no monsters to scare me. "The princess sleeps until the prince kisses her. But you don't deserve her. I do."

But just as I said them, my words rang hollow. I could not awaken the princess; I had tried. And even if I had, would she have consented to marry me? No. I was thinking only about myself, and not about my love.

Better for her to be awake than lost in unending sleep.

"She's this way," I said, dejected. I should have known I could never achieve my dream. Men like me never do.

I led him to her room where she slept. "Here she is," I said. "But treat her well—"

From somewhere in his cloak he pulled out a wooden stake and a hammer.

"What do you need that for?" I asked.

"What do you think? To kill the bitch."

I could not conceive of wanting to kill that beauty. "What? Why?"

"She is a monster. She rises in the night and preys on the village. The thorns were there to keep her inside, but they do no good."

"She has slept all these years. I have never seen her awake."

"Have you seen her at night?" the prince asked.

He was right. I did not like the night, with its noises and darkness. I stayed away from the palace, safe in my room. "No," I said. "But I sleep in a room here in the castle. If she were a monster surely I would be one of her easier victims. Why is that?"

"Cretin. It's the garlic. You reek of it!"

"Garlic?" I liked it in my cooking, and kept some hanging near the kitchen door.

He advanced on the princess. "Leave her alone!" I shouted.

"Stop being so stupid." He had the stake in his hand, and a mallet in the other, ready to plunge it into her heart.

But I barely saw. "Stupid" he called me. The word hurt like a lash on my back, like salt on a bleeding gash. It had not lost its power to wound me, even after so long a time.

Years of rage that I didn't even know I had bubbled up in me.

My hands, strong from work, grasped his neck, pressing, pressing, pressing. Harder, harder. "I am not stupid," I shouted, screaming in his ear and I felt him grasping for breath. "*I am not stupid.*"

When my frenzy was over, he was limp. I tossed him onto the stone floor, the back of his skull hitting it with the satisfying thump, like a melon against a rock.

I stared at him. The stake had fallen atop the princess. I tossed it off into a corner.

I leaned over at her. It was several hours until nightfall. No matter.

I gave her a kiss, long and hard, tasting blood on her red lips.

She stirred, just a bit. One eye opened.

"I will be ready for you, my princess," I said. "In my room by the kitchen."

Her eye shut again.

I left the room, kicking the prince just to show him that I was no fool. He made no sound.

Overjoyed, I returned to my room, and tore away every last morsel of garlic. Then I lay on my pallet to await the princess's kiss.

It would be like a fairy tale.

On a Clear Day You Can See All the Way to Conspiracy by Desmond Warzel [sci-fi]

You're listening to the Mike Colavito Show on Cleveland's home for straight talk, WCUY 1200. The opinions expressed on this program do not reflect those of WCUY, its management, or its sponsors.

Fair warning; I'm in a mood today, folks.

We've got a mayor whose only talent seems to be showing up at luncheons and waving at the cameras.

Eighty bucks I had to pay yesterday for not wearing my seatbelt. Show me the seatbelts on a school bus.

I saw a Cleveland athlete on national TV last night wearing a Yankees cap.

And every day I get at least a dozen calls from schmucks who think that people like me are the problem in this city.

Tell me America's not falling apart.

[pause]

And some of you people--including our programming director, by the way--seem to think I'm running my mouth too much and not taking enough phone calls. I've only been number one in radio in this city for ten straight years; what would I know?

You want calls? You got 'em. Steven in Mayfield Heights, you're on the air.

"Hey, what's up, Mike?"

The rent. Art in Seven Hills, you're on WCUY.

"How you doing, Mike. Just wondering if you caught that ball game last night?"

No. Andrea in Rocky River, go ahead.

"Hi, Mike, first-time caller."

Well, call back tomorrow and you'll be a second-time caller. Carol in Cleveland, what's on your mind?

"Mike, what do you think of waterboarding?"

My wife and I waterboard all the time, and it's improved our sex life dramatically. Chuck in Parma, you're on the air.

"Hey, Mike, I heard your show yesterday, and I was just wondering, if you know so much about football, why *you* don't take over as head coach of the Browns?"

I wouldn't want to take the pay cut. Mina in Lakewood, you're on the air.

"Does your wife think that waterboarding crack was funny?"

Play your cards right some night and you could find out for yourself, Mina. Tommy in Beachwood, you're on WCUY.

"Hi, Mike, just wondering who you think the Indians should try and trade for next year."

Your mother. Jane in Euclid, go ahead.

[pause]

Looks like we lost Jane in Euclid. Must have answered her question already. That's all right; we got in seven callers in under a minute. Everyone happy now? Hey, Jake, I have to take a breather; do the traffic.

What?

Oh, yeah. This traffic is brought to you by West Side Hardware.

Thanks, Mike. Not much happening right now; 480, 271, and 77 are all clear, but traffic on the Shoreway is backed up in both directions, so our listeners might want to allow a few extra minutes if they're headed that way. For West Side Hardware, this has been your WCUY traffic report on Cleveland's home for straight talk.

Hey, Jake, don't go yet. You still there? I gotta take the Shoreway home after the show. Any idea what the holdup is?

Can't say, Mike; no accidents, just a general slowdown all along the lakeshore.

Wonderful.

And people wonder why I'm always giving the mayor grief. Straightest stretch of highway in America, and traffic still won't move. Somebody on the Shoreway, call in and tell me what the hell's going on over there. Franklin in Cleveland, you're on the air.

"What's up, Mike? You gonna let me talk?"

Don't worry, it's all out of my system. The floor's yours.

"Well, you're entitled to your opinion about the mayor, but come on, man, how you gonna blame him for slow traffic?"

The traffic's just a symptom. I'm talking about neglect. Name me one thing the mayor's accomplished since he took office.

"Well--"

You can't, Franklin, because there are none. Homicides in the triple digits, a downtown that looks like Baghdad, none of it bothers him. Everything's A-OK as long as his picture's on the front page every day.

"In fairness, Mike, he didn't *create* those problems, he inherited most of them--"

Gotta let you go, Franklin, I think we've got an answer to my traffic query on line two. Pete on the Shoreway, what's happening over there?

"There's no wreck or anything, Mike; I think everyone's just slowing down to look at the sky."

The sky?

"Bunch of jet trails over Lake Erie."

Jet trails? I'm gonna be late for my poker game tonight because a bunch of morons are staring at *jet trails*? You people never seen a jet trail before?

"Well, there's one hell of a lot of them; must be hundreds going every which way. I've never seen anything like it. Might be military planes--they're looping and weaving all over the place."

Okay, thanks, Pete. Now hang up the phone and pay attention before you kill someone.

[pause]

Well, if there's anyone left listening after this fascinating line of inquiry, in the next hour we'll be talking to the Indians' hitting coach...

How's that?

All right, one more. Mel on the Shoreway, go ahead, you're on the air.

"Hi, Mike. Hey, if you could see this for yourself, you might not dismiss it so fast. You think anybody else in the Cleveland media is going to bother looking into it?"

You're right about that. But listen, you don't think this might just be regular air traffic?

"Well, one of them just flew straight up, so you tell me."

Thanks, Mel.

Okay, I have no window and I can't leave, so somebody out there take some pictures of these things and email 'em to me during the ad break. Meanwhile, I'll run down the hall to our WCUY news department and lean on those clowns, see if they know anything. Let's get to the bottom of this so we can move on.

[break]

And we're back on the Mike Colavito Show, where we're devoting fifty thousand watts to a discussion of jet trails, if you can believe it. Thanks to our listeners, I've now seen some pictures of this mess, and, as much as it pains me, I have to agree with those people out on the Shoreway; that's no ordinary air traffic.

And, I just checked with our newsroom; they have no clue. No surprise there, they haven't broken a story since Teapot Dome. Guess we'll just have to wait and see. Anyhow, unless you have something new to add, no more calls about this, okay? We know what it looks like. Craig in Mentor, you're on the air.

"Have you seen the sky this afternoon, Mike? You should see what's going on up there!"

Richard in Dayton...Dayton? Really? Well, thanks for listening all the way down there, Richard. Hey, at least you're not calling about the sky over Lake Erie, right?

"Actually, Mr. Colavito, that's exactly what I'm calling about."

You mean this is going on in Dayton, too?

"Well, Mr. Colavito--"

Call me Mike, we're all friends here.

"Mike, I'm not in Dayton proper; I'm calling from Wright-Patterson."

The Air Force base?

"Yes sir, and I just wanted to clarify for your listening audience that there is no unusual aviation activity over northeastern Ohio."

None at all?

"No sir."

That's official?

"Yes sir."

So does that mean all those jet trails are from commercial planes after all?

"Absolutely."

Richard, I might have been born on a Monday, but it wasn't last Monday.

"Mike, the air traffic's always like that; but between the clouds and the pollution, you just can't see it most of the time. Sometimes, though, when the weather's cold and the sky's clear enough, those trails become visible."

And that's all it is?

"That's all, Mike."

There are a lot of planes up there, Richard.

"It may look like it, but it's perfectly normal."

Well, I appreciate your call, sir.

"Any time, Mike. I'm just doing my duty, which in this case means averting a potential panic before it gets started."

Thanks again, Richard.

[pause]

Cold weather and a clear sky, gimme a break. No way I'm falling for this. Ronnie in Solon, you're on the air.

"Hey Mike, maybe we're being invaded by Canada."

Could be, Ronnie; they were probably pretty peeved when the Indians swept the Blue Jays last week. Jeannie in South Euclid, you're on WCUY.

"They might be flying saucers, Mike, had you considered that?"

Anyone smart enough to get to Earth would know better than to look for intelligent life in Cleveland. Look, I know Jeannie's kidding, but let's nip this stuff in the bud, okay? I don't need those kinds of people coming out of the woodwork. John in Ashtabula, you're on the air.

"Hi, Mike. Listen, I wouldn't go dismissing this alien theory out of hand if I were you. It just so happens I'm an extraterrestrial myself."

Oh, is that a fact? Now we're getting somewhere. And when did you land here in Ohio?

"Oh, I didn't land in the United States; I landed in Mexico and snuck across. Much easier that way."

Never be funnier than the host, John. Jules in Cleveland Heights, go ahead.

"Mike, I don't know what's going on up there, but I can only hope it *is* aliens. I think we've gone as far as can on our own, and our only hope for peace and harmony is the descent of a new wisdom."

[pause]

Well, you're definitely from Cleveland Heights, there's no doubt about that. Go ahead, Jules.

"Humans have lost the way. We need to evolve and we're stuck fast. Did you know we only use ten percent of our brains? Imagine if we could learn to harness all of our potential!"

Hey, Jules, guess what? People use a hundred percent of their brains all the time. It's called a seizure, dummy.

I've already cut you off, Jules, but if you're still listening, let me help you out, buddy; I think you hit the wrong button on your radio this afternoon. You want the one marked FM. This is AM, and it's not safe for you here.

Let's go to commercial, we've got bills to pay.

[break]

And we're back, with certainly the oddest show I've ever done in ten years of radio. We've been discussing what I suspect are military jets in enormous numbers over Lake Erie, and I'm under the impression some people would rather we didn't talk about it. There's more to this than meets the eye, folks.

William in Dayton...another caller from Dayton? I suppose you're in the Air Force too?

"Mr. Colavito, we've already explained the situation adequately. You'd be well-advised to stop spreading misinformation, let the matter drop altogether, and continue your show with a different topic."

What's that, a threat?

Hello?

Well, you can forget it, William, or whatever your real name is, I'll talk about it until morning if I feel like it. If something dangerous is happening, we've got a right to know. You'll have to drag me out of this studio.

You think I'm afraid of the government? You think I have skeletons in my closet? All my skeletons are arranged tastefully on the front lawn. Patrick in Gates Mills, you're on the air.

"Hello, Mike?"

Go ahead, Patrick.

"Mike, I think I can clarify this entire situation for everyone, but I'll need you to bear with me."

I'm begging you, Patrick. I'm all ears.

"Thank you, Mike. Now, I have to begin by saying that I am not originally from this planet--"

Stop right there.

"Yes, Mike?"

[sigh]

All right, let me tell you something, Patrick, this better get real interesting real fast. If you're just some everyday nut, call back after midnight when that UFO guy comes on. You got me?

"I promise to make it worth your while, Mike."

See that you do, Patrick.

"Perhaps this story would be more palatable if I spoke hypothetically. Suppose a person was in possession of some sensitive information--a new technology, say, or a military secret, or just some dirt on a politician--that, in the right hands, could change galactic civilization forever…"

Galactic civilization? Look, I'm not much of a Trekkie, Patrick. I only watch baseball, wrestling, and Rachael Ray.

"And suppose…Rachael Ray? Really?"

Get on with it, Patrick.

"And suppose you wanted this person out of the way, but he had a high enough profile that he couldn't simply be done away with. What would you do? What *could* you do? Hide him in plain sight, on a crowded but unsophisticated planet, where no one could attempt to contact or rescue him without endangering his life. And he would have no choice but to adjust to his exile, to try and blend in with the barbarians, because even if he told the truth to everyone he met, no one would believe him."

And this hypothetical alien is you, I suppose?

"That's correct. I appreciate your open-mindedness."

No problem, Patrick. Do you look human? You blending in okay?

"My disguise has been effective so far."

What do you really look like?

"That's hard to describe, at least in English."

Well, thanks for outing yourself, so to speak, here on the Mike Colavito Show. But what's it got to do with anything?

"Those flying saucers over the lake--and that is indeed what they are, not jet planes--represent a rather ill-advised attempt by some of my more zealous supporters to effect my rescue."

Patrick?

"Yes, Mike?"

That's about as plausible as anything else I've heard today. But why reveal yourself now?

"Well, since the military is obviously monitoring your show, I thought perhaps an explanation of my situation might convince them not to interfere. Despite my present situation, I still have some rather powerful friends, and if something should happen to those spacecraft, even through a misunderstanding, it might not bode well for this planet, which, I must say, I've grown rather fond of."

And I'm sure the feeling's mutual, Patrick. Can you hang on through the break? This is the most fun I've had in a long time.

"I should really go, Mike; I've revealed too much already, and I've certainly placed myself in danger. But thank you for hearing me out."

God love you, Patrick, you've made my afternoon.

[break]

If you're just joining us, we've been discussing the plethora of jet trails over northeastern Ohio this afternoon, despite objections from certain quarters, and our most amusing theory comes from an apparent extraterrestrial living out in Gates Mills. If anybody can top it, I'm all ears. Ahmed in Lyndhurst, you're on the air.

"Yes, Mike, I wanted to talk to you about Patrick; the last caller? Don't believe a word he said; that story was nothing but a pack of lies."

Congratulations on figuring that out, Ahmed. I was just having a little harmless fun by going along with him. What's the problem?

"Harmless is hardly the word I would use to describe the most nefarious criminal in the galaxy, Mike."

Oh, boy.

I asked for it, I guess. Much as I'd like to just go home right now and ride out the invasion in my media room, I guess you better elaborate.

"Naturally. Hypothetically speaking, suppose there were a master criminal of such malevolent cunning, with a network of felonious associates so vast, that anything he set his sights on was as good as his. Such a person could conceivably be responsible for the misappropriation of thousands of valuable items: state treasures, art objects, anything he could find a buyer for. Eventually there would be no option for a moral society but to banish him to a planet where, from a galactic standpoint, there was nothing worth stealing. No offense."

None taken, Ahmed. And how do you know this?

"Well, one could never set such a dangerous person loose on a primitive planet without also leaving a minder behind to keep an eye on things. It would be unethical."

And this minder, that's you, right?

"That's correct."

So you are also an alien?

"That's right, Mike."

And the trails?

"They're spacecraft, just as Patrick said."

He was telling the truth about that?

"I'm not scheduled to be relieved of my post here for another five years, so it can only be his cronies trying to extract him. I'm sure Patrick would like nothing better than for you to believe that he's a political prisoner; he seems to think Earth is peopled entirely by rubes. I don't, which is why I'm entrusting you with the truth. And I would also advise your Air Force to go ahead and engage those spacecraft; their destruction would be to the general good, and an immeasurable favor to Earth."

I wonder if we could get Patrick back on for a rebuttal. Anything else to add, Ahmed?

"That's it, Mike. Strictly speaking, I've said too much, but I think it's for the best. I couldn't just sit idly by."

And we appreciate it, Ahmed. What do you think of our planet?

"I've seen worse. I do like the food."

Thanks, Ahmed.

[pause]

Wow.

Is it time for the news yet?

Well, we still have a few minutes before the news break. Time for one more call. Maybe the Air Force'll call back.

Line one's lit up, but there's no name or city. Hey, screener; who's on line one?

What do you mean you don't know?

Christ, I gotta do everything myself, I guess.

Okay, you're on the air on WCUY; who am I talking to?

Hello?

"I enjoyed hearing from Patrick and Ahmed very much, but I've got a story that's even better. Are you interested?"

Sure, what have I got to lose? But who--

"Imagine a galactic civilization of unknowable antiquity, lapsed into decadence after eons of peace.

"Imagine a race from elsewhere, born of darkness but covetous of the light, desirous of exterminating the galaxy's present inhabitants and assuming their place, but so unimaginably patient as to postpone invasion for nearly an eternity, until their evolution assured their practical invincibility.

"Such a race, attacking from all sides and from within, might very well eliminate all traces of galactic culture in mere hours.

"They might then take their time surveying the uncivilized worlds, calculating which species might best be enslaved and which simply eradicated.

"It is conceivable that on one such marginal planet, they might discover two remnants of the newly-extinct civilization; a convict and his jailor, perhaps.

"Fastidious to a fault, they would insist on destroying these last two anachronistic relics of a dead society, though, not entirely lacking a sense of humor, they might first take them back to their native worlds and show them what had been wrought in their absence.

"Knowing that others of their race would eventually return to this planet when its fate was determined, their innate orderliness would dictate that no evidence of this visit remain. To this end, a tailored but relatively simple signal, delivered simultaneously on all communication frequencies, would readily excise all offending memories from the natives' unsophisticated brains, leaving them once again blissfully ignorant.

"All hypothetically speaking, of course. May I ask what you think of my story?"

Not much, I'm afraid. Good delivery, but lacks panache. I appreciate your call, though--

What is that? Does anyone else hear that?

That noise, it's going right up my spine. Are we broadcasting that? What the hell...

[pause]

What was that?

[pause]

What were we talking about? Should we take a call? I have no idea what's going on...

[pause]

Okay, it's time for WCUY's award-winning news, then we'll talk to the Cleveland Indians' hitting coach and see if we can't iron out this trouble they've been having. Back in a few...

Afternoon Break by Gregg Chamberlain [sci-fi]

It only seems like it's always full-moon night at the Tesseract. Even in broad daylight.

I was on the first week of my three weeks' allotment of vacation time at the paper. So, early Friday afternoon, I dropped by the pub for a half-pint before taking in one of the matinees at the Mayfair. I was thinking maybe the latest Avengers or else something animated.

Ernie and Raj were at the corner chess table, studying the board. Sky and the hobbit hovered over them, critiquing the game and offering advice on moves. A few other regulars occupied tables, enjoying a quiet afternoon glass while chatting or just contemplating the air.

Perched on my own stool at the end of the bar, I watched as Shale slowly drew off my mug full of Wolfshead draft. He was just picking up the steel ruler to swipe off the foam when the front door banged open.

Everyone looked up, squinting at the bright high-noon rectangle of light. In through the door, out of Vancouver's July heatwave, rushed this manic-looking guy, dressed up in what I guess you might call Mad Max modern, complete to a pair of goggles shoved up high on his forehead.

Wild eyes stared around the room. Fixed on Shale, standing behind the bar.

"Quick!" he shouted. "What year is this?"

Shale answered without a moment's hesitation. "It's 2014, dude."

The stranger stomped a foot and cursed. "Damn it! Calibration's still off!"

He spun around and, still muttering loudly about "temporal vectors" and "coding glitches", stomped back out the door and disappeared into the sidewalk traffic.

We all watched as the door slowly swung shut. Blinked our eyes and then went back to what we were doing before the interruption. I turned to find Shale just finishing flicking the foam off the ruler while at the same time handing over my half-pint mug.

He looked back over towards the door and shook his head. "Third time this year," he said with a shrug.

The Monster In Me by Suzie Lockhart/ Bruce Lockhart 2nd [horror]

Randall Bell stared up at the ceiling fan rotating slowly above his head, afraid to move. He allowed his eyes to roam around the unfamiliar area. Bright sunlight streamed through a window to his left, making little particles of dust visible as they floated in the air. The curtains on the window featured an apple pattern trimmed in a sickly green. A variety of herbs sat drying out on the window ledge. A horde of flies was buzzing around.

Randall slowly moved his head, his nose wrinkling from the strange, yet familiar, odor assaulting his nostrils, while he eyed the rest of the small, but tidy, kitchen. Oh, God, he thought, please not again.

What the stench was he could only guess at; he didn't plan on sticking around to find out. He sat up, checking to make sure he wasn't hurt before grabbing onto the edge of the kitchen counter and pulling himself to his feet. Silently, he padded over to the door further down on his left, resisting the urge to look at what undoubtedly would be a gruesome scene. He squinted against the brilliant sunshine as he quietly stepped out, holding one hand over his eyes. In the driveway Randall's vanilla-white SUV awaited, and he sighed in relief at the sight. At least he had his car. Reaching in the pocket of his suit, he discovered his car keys. Also inside his suit jacket was his cell phone. He took it out and turned away from the sun to check the screen. A surge of panic shot through him when he saw the date.

Randall Bell had just lost three days.

He couldn't remember a damn thing, except feeling that familiar tightening in his throat while drinking Irish whiskey at a local bar. A particularly tough case was finally over, and he'd been celebrating with his colleagues when he felt it rise up into his chest, squeezing the air out of his lungs. He coughed up blood into a napkin, and then excused himself.

Randall didn't attempt to recall what might've happened during the missing seventy some hours. His instincts assured him that the less he knew the better. Especially after what happened last time.

So instead he drove around until he came across a sign pointing towards the Pennsylvania Turnpike. To his dismay, he saw that he was about one hundred miles from his home near Harrisburg.

He pushed his SUV up to seventy miles per hour. He just wanted to get home and put this reoccurring nightmare behind him. Of course, he couldn't…not really, when vivid flashes of doing things, horrible things, permeated his thoughts.

Then there was the receipt for odd items he didn't remember buying, like Italian leather shoes and a hunting knife. What scared Randall the most were the things he'd read about in the papers. That was why he'd avoided hospitals; evidence. He was terrified of being connected to the crime scenes.

The sun continued to beat down so Randall cranked up the air conditioner. He felt the now familiar squirming sensation deep in his gut. He was about half way to his destination when…

"Ugh!" he groaned from the sudden pain in his intestines. He pulled into the Blue Mountain Service station and ran to the men's room. As Randall sat on the toilet, he bit his lip until it bled; due to the pain he was experiencing as whatever food he didn't recall eating was violently purged. Tears squeezed out from behind his eyelids, and he wondered if this was similar to the pain during childbirth.

If so, Randall now had a new respect for women.

He knew he would not make it home before another blackout hit. Randall grabbed some Tums and a pack of gum, asking at the checkout if anyone knew where the nearest hospital was.

It had been a dull afternoon at Blue Ridge Hospital when a handsome stranger in a rumpled, but expensive-looking, business suit walked up to the window of the nurse's office of the Emergency Room, breaking the monotony. Up to that point in her double shift, Michelle Dawson, R.N., had dealt with nothing out of the ordinary. A girl who drank too much at a fraternity party, a guy having some seriously nasty withdrawal from his crack pipe, and a little girl with a broken finger.

"Name?" She inquired pleasantly.

"Randall Bell." As she looked up and the man moved closer, Michelle noticed his features appeared strained, and beads of sweat had formed on his brow.

"What can we help you with today, Mr. Bell? Are you running a fever?" She motioned for him to come inside her triage station. He sank down in a chair immediately, letting out a small grunt. Michelle pulled on a pair of purple nitrile gloves and took a thermometer out of a drawer, as a woman from the reception area joined them to ask the usual litany of questions. After slipping it inside the plastic sleeve, Michelle popped the thermometer in his mouth.

Upon hearing the beep, she saw that, indeed, Randall Bell was running a slight fever, 99.5.

She waited a little impatiently for the young girl to check his I.D. and insurance card. She hated when they asked for patient's co-pays up front; a sick person shouldn't have to go through that. Randall pulled a gold card out of his leather wallet and handed to the receptionist, who bustled away to get approval.

"Sorry about that." Michelle preferred not to follow generally accepted protocol, because she felt a sick person should be seen by the triage nurse first. The 'higher-ups' didn't like it, and she didn't care. She was a good nurse, had been here in the E.R. for ten years now. "You're running a bit of a temperature, Mr. Bell." Michelle smiled at him. Even in his present state, he was a very nice looking man. "Would you please take off your suit jacket so I can get your blood pressure?"

He nodded and struggled out of the Copenhagen blue jacket that must've cost a pretty penny. She wondered what he did for a living. She'd felt the taunt muscles of his arm underneath his pale blue shirt when she strapped on the cuff.

Time to put a halt to the direction her thoughts were taking. She was supposed to be a professional, after all.

His blood pressure was definitely too high for a man of his age and physical condition and his pulse was rapid, as well. Her brows creased together.

"What is bothering you this evening, Mr. Bell?"

Randall Bell sat tight-lipped, unsure of how to tell this nice nurse exactly what his problem was. He cleared his throat. "I... I don't know how to explain this." She would never believe him. Hell, he certainly didn't want to believe it.

Except, he did. In one of those fragmented memories, he was looking in a mirror, but staring back at him was an evil, monstrous face.

"Try your best." She encouraged. How unusual that such a successful looking gentleman could not articulate what, exactly, was wrong. Then again, most men did hate admitting anything was wrong. Hated doctors, period.

The nurse tending to him had a beautiful smile; Randall thought she was a few steps shy of looking like Halle Berry. A light citrus scent lingered on her honey skin. A fleeting thought ran through his mind; he wondered what had made her want to become a nurse.

"I've been in a lot of pain. I have trouble falling asleep. I..." Randall wondered how to explain the blackouts.

"I see. Tell me, where does it hurt?" Michelle asked.

He stared into eyes the color of amber, thick lashes curling around them. "All over."

"Hmm, like a flu bug?"

He shook his head no, trying to convey his ailment without sounding totally off his rocker. "I have these blackouts. I wake up in strange places. It's getting really bad, affecting my work."

"What do you do?"

"I'm an attorney." Randall Bell replied, hesitant to tell her he was the state's prosecutor. This could be really bad for him. His career would be over.

Michelle's eyes widened a bit. A bit of chemistry lingered in the air between them. He could feel it. But he could also feel...

"Ugh, ow!" Randall hollered out in pain, doubling over and clutching his stomach.

The nurse was hovering over him, and when the pain subsided, she wanted to check his abdomen. She helped him onto the examination table, asking him to lift his shirt.

Damn, Michelle thought, as she pressed gently on his rock-hard abs. Even her slight touch made him squirm and wince. "I'm sorry," she murmured, right before coming across an odd lump. When she pressed on it, it moved. Shocked, she backed away just as Randall cried out.

"What... I mean, how long..." Unexpectedly, she found herself at a loss for words.

Randall turned to look at her. Unwelcome tears were streaming down his cheeks from the agony. He had to tell her... had to tell somebody.

"I... I just lost three days. I need a surgeon to... to get out this monster that's inside of me!"

Michelle stood shell-shocked for a moment. He had to be using the word monster as a metaphor. Great, she thought, a super-hot guy comes in and he might be a nut case. She took out a chart and began writing, trying to mask her disappointment, but at the same time wondering what the hell was in there, moving around.

"Um... okay, Mr. Bell. Can you elaborate? Tell me when this started. Please."

"Several weeks ago."

Michelle wasn't sure she wanted to know more. He might be really ill, or really sick in the head. Either way, she decided to let the doctors sort it out.

"Okay, Mr. Bell. I'm going to send you right back to room 4B, and we'll order some blood work and x-rays." She attempted to keep her voice steady.

He lay back on the bed. "I'm not nuts. There really is a monster in, ugh, me." It was apparent that Randall's pain was getting worse. Michelle would talk to the E.R. doctor about giving him something to ease his discomfort.

She put her hand gently on his arm and tried to sound reassuring. "We'll get this all figured out. Just try to take it easy."

He winced again, briefly placing his hand over hers. "You're very pretty, you know. Thank you."

She patted his hand for a moment before pulling away uncertainly, and then she called for a wheelchair to take him back.

Randall hated emergency rooms. Who didn't? The noise, the God-awful gowns, and the smells especially disgusted him. Of course, they weren't as bad as what he'd smelled earlier at that strange house. He could hear doctors and nurses whispering outside his room. He knew they thought he was a nut case, but there was also concern that something was definitely amiss. The nurse had felt the damn thing move. Every time it shifted, the pain was excruciating. A young man had come in to take blood about a half hour before. Randall had been left alone since.

"Mr. Bell?" An older nurse dressed in a traditional starched white dress, complete with the hat on her head, came bustling in. "We're going to take you back for an MRI."

Randall nodded. He could just imagine the look on the doctor's face when the doctor saw what was inside of him.

He was asked the usual questions, including if he was allergic to iodine. They felt the contrast dye would help reveal what was going on.

"Where is the pain located?"

At the moment, it was still in his gut, but felt as though it was trying to make its way up into his chest. He circled the whole area with a finger. He was given a Dixie cup with 4 ounces of something comparable to cough syrup, but more disgusting, to drink.

A male technician named Tyler was waiting for him in a small, sterile room. The tech helped him onto a table, speaking to him in a calming tone of voice.

Randall wasn't very comfortable; it was not made for a six-foot-tall man.

"We also need to add some contrast through your I.V."

The dye seared through his veins and made him feel slightly nauseous.

"This won't take long, Mr. Bell. Close your eyes and try to relax." The machine began whirring and the table lifted slightly as it entered the giant donut hole. Tyler stood beside him, pressing a few buttons on the side of the donut, reassuring Randall that even though he would be in the small room off to the side, he would be able to hear and see him, in case there were any problems.

His arms dangled off the table above his head. The machine clicked as Randall was moved to and fro through the opening. The sound echoed around him infuriatingly.

He tried to remain still, but he couldn't help crying out from the pain.

"Are you okay, Mr. Bell?" The irritatingly calm voice asked.

"Spectacular." Sarcasm laced his tone.

The bed returned to its resting position, and Randall was helped into a wheelchair. God, how he hated all of this; being treated like some invalid.

"Augh!" He hollered, doubling over. Damn this thing!

As he was led back to 4B, Randall Bell could feel the nasty creature crawling around in him, scraping its claws against every fiber of his being, as if it was trying to figure out just what made him tick.

He was emotionally and physically drained. What did that damned thing do when it forced Randall to black-out?

The pulsating entity was pushing its way up his esophagus again, and when he felt his throat tighten and the breath being knocked out of him, he tried to let out a terrified scream.

There was a flurry of activity as the doctor rushed in. Randall's throat looked swollen. He heard someone say through his haze of confusion, that they thought he was having an allergic reaction to the iodine. He tried gesturing with his hands, but they were busy shooting medication into him to counteract the reaction he wasn't even having.

Blood spewed from his mouth, splattering the doctor. Randall was howling in agony.

"Dilaudid. Stat!" The older nurse that had been there earlier handed the doctor a clean towel. A younger girl beside her hurried after the doctor, and came back within minutes, handing the older nurse a syringe.

"Mr. Bell, this is Dilaudid. It's for the pain."

Some relief would be nice. There was sincere concern etched on her wrinkled face. He wasn't aware that his eyes were bulging.

The hairs on the back of his neck stood on end as a prickling sensation briefly overwhelmed him Then a wave of warmth washed through him, and his body began to relax.

"There, there," the older nurse cooed at him as if he were a baby. At thirty-five, to her maybe he was. He was feeling fuzzy. That dil… dila… whatever the hell it was, it was some good shit, he thought. Even the monster seemed to settle. Randall wondered if the thing was just biding its time.

"Thank you," he murmured drowsily.

The nurse left the room, and the menace inside Randall Bell began to slither up his brain stem.

When he stood, Randall Bell was a little woozy at first. It took an extra minute or two to gather himself enough to get dressed. By the time he straightened his cuffs and tied the laces on his Italian shoes, he was perfectly fine.

Or, rather, IT was. Bell was sound asleep.

Hmmm, now where was that delicious nurse that had greeted him earlier? What was her name? Michelle something…?

Two doctors stared at the films from Randall Bell's CT. Their logical minds not fully comprehending the images of the horrific face staring back at them.

"Dedicated to Terry—a loving soul gone to soon."

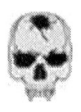

Spare Change by Chuck Rothman [fantasy]

"Spare change?" Roger asked.

The man walked just a bit faster, not even making eye contact.

"Have a good evening, sir," Roger added. He coughed and pulled his worn trenchcoat tighter. October already. Soon it would be winter again, and he wasn't sure if he could survive the cold.

Florida. That would be such a relief, especially since they ordered the shelters not to take him in. But last year they wouldn't let him leave New York. There were breakdowns and delayed trains. Not even hitchhiking had worked, though the 30 days in jail had been a relief. They had been very thorough, but, then, they always were. They plotted against him, taking his job and just about everything else from him.

Three years ago, he'd been working for Chase. Now he was begging in the street in a coat you could practically see through, and hoping he wouldn't have to face another New York winter. His sinuses were already killing him where the chip had been implanted. They had done all this to him and he had no idea why.

Another man was approaching. Maybe today they'd let him get a few dollars. Roger could never be sure when someone said "no" if it was just bad luck, or because people were being told to avoid him. Or maybe a combination. The rules always seemed to be changing. Begging was the only thing they ever let him do. Probably because of the constant humiliation.

"Spare change, mister?" he said.

The man smiled and tossed a couple of quarters his way. "Why certainly, Roger. And that's just the start."

Roger jolted at the sound of his name. It had been months since anyone used it. He tried to place the man. He was medium height, and wore an Italian suit that probably cost more than Roger had managed to scrape together in three years of begging. Maybe they had met back when he still worked at the bank. But that was so long ago, before they had done this too him. "You know me?"

"Of course, Roger. We've been following you with a lot of interest."

Then Roger understood. "You're one of them, aren't you?"

The man nodded. "Smart man, Roger. We like that. You can call me Smith, if you like. How'd you like to be treated to lunch at the Bernadin?"

Roger laughed. He knew of the place, one of the fanciest in the city. "They won't even let me walk by the place. They're not going to let me inside looking like this."

Smith only smiled.

The maitre d' didn't give Roger a second glance as he seated the two men. No mention of even wearing a tie. No mention of the fact Roger hadn't had a shower in ages. Just a seat in the best table in the restaurant.

"Try the lamb," the man said as he picked up the menu.

Roger glanced at the items. "I don't see it."

His host just grinned. "You're with me. They'll serve it."

Roger set down the menu. "All right, what's this all about?"

"I think you get the general idea."

"You did all this to me, that I know. Who are you?"

"The official name is the Technological Hierarchy for the Education of Mankind, but we prefer call ourselves 'Them.' It cuts down on confusion."

"So you're one big conspiracy. Like the Kennedy assassination."

"Oh, please," Smith said. "We had nothing to do with *that*; Jack was one of us. No one gets to be President without us; I can tell you the results of the next three presidential elections, if you want. We've been running things since the '40s."

"Everything?"

Smith nodded. "Everything. That's why we were able to do all this to you."

"Tell my parents I was dead?"

"We even supplied the body for the funeral."

"And my friends?"

"You know the answer to that."

Roger did. When he tried to call, the phones wouldn't work. When he tried to drive, the car wouldn't start—when he had a car. When he walked to a friend's apartment, he'd been arrested. Once the entire apartment building where his ex-girlfriend lived was missing.

"Yeah," Roger said. "I guess I do. But why me? I can't see how I could have been any threat to you."

"Threat?" Smith started to laugh. "*Threat?*" The laughter was strong and loud now. It went on for several minutes before he managed to get control of himself. "Of course you're not a threat. We control *everything*, so there's nothing you can do to threaten us."

Roger faced the guffaws with a growing sense of irritation. "Then why?"

"We have nothing to challenge us. We need something to amuse ourselves, to stay sharp. That's why we invented the Game."

"The Game?"

"Think of it as a form of tag. You will choose the next person to suddenly lose everything. At that point, you're free."

"To do what? Starve?"

"Oh, I think you'll manage. You were one of the best, really. Nearly three years without cracking. Some of us will be happy give you a hand getting your heart's desire."

"What do you mean?"

Smith took out a magazine. "Been to the movies much?"

"Other than using one as a place to flop? Of course not."

"Pity. You'll have a lot to catch up with." He opened the magazine and pointed to a picture.

It was an ad for a film. *Blinding Justice* was the name. Starring Kris Flynn. "So?"

"Take a closer look."

Roger did. The face was familiar, even if the name was not.

Then it registered.

"My God. It's her!"

Smith nodded.

Roger had never known her name. She was just a panhandler hitting him up for spare change. He remembered wondering why she was on the street. Something about her made her seem out of place.

He took pity on her and gave her a fifty.

She had looked at the bill in disbelief. "I'm not a hooker," she finally said, reluctantly handing the bill back to him.

"I know. Keep it. It's a gift."

She rubbed it several times, as though expecting it to vanish. "Thank you," she said, tears in her eyes. "Oh, thank you. If ever there was an angel on Earth, you're it."

Roger had smiled.

But she had turned pale. "Oh, God," she said. "Oh, God. I didn't mean it. I didn't mean *him*!" Then she turned to Roger. "I'm sorry, so very sorry."

Roger had rushed away, thinking his assessment of her sanity was a little too rash.

A week later, they implanted the chip in his nose and it all began.

Roger looked up from the picture. "You did this to her? A beggar?"

"How do you think she ended up a beggar in the first place?" Smith placed his napkin on his lap. "She had played very well, so she got what she wanted most. What do you want most, Roger?"

What I want, thought Roger, was to wipe that grin off your face. "I don't know."

"Well, you can decide that later. You have a more important decision first. You need to choose our next subject."

"Me?"

"Exactly. You must choose someone, knowing full well that he will have his life destroyed. It's your responsibility."

"No, it isn't."

"Oh, you can always decide not to choose anyone. You can continue living like you have. I guarantee you won't be eating dinner at the Bernadin, that's for sure." Smith gave another one of his goddamn smiles. "And the one way to recover your life is to choose. Just say 'you're it' and you'll pick the next victim. You'll just sneeze out the chip and be on your way." He sipped from the water glass. "I'd suggest you choose someone who thinks himself a big success. Someone smug and self-satisfied. They're always the most fun to watch."

"Someone like you?"

Smith nodded. "That's the spirit. Get out all that anger. Maybe there's some banker or rich man who looks like me. You can get a vicarious revenge."

Roger had no use for a vicarious revenge right then. "Why not the real thing?" he asked, realizing he had the perfect answer. "You're it."

Smith laughed. "I'm afraid others have tried that. No, the rules are it can't be one of us."

Roger's felt like he had fallen down a well.

"So who are you going to choose? Who are you going to condemn to this fate? I admit I find this part of the game the most fascinating. Will you go for revenge on some poor slob who crosses you? Will you try to be noble, until you are so starved that nobility seems beside the point? Will you do it accidentally, like poor Kris? There are so many options."

"You bastard!"

"Yes, I *am* one, aren't I?" Smith's laugh was practically a giggle. "But you don't have to decide right now. Take your time. Think about it. It's more entertaining that way."

"That's all human lives are to you?" Roger was almost shouting, but no one in the restaurant even looked that way. "Entertainment?"

"Of course, Roger," Smith said, obviously enjoying Roger's anger. "What else?"

The waiter arrived, a bottle of wine in his hand. "Compliments of the management," he said.

"Of course," said Smith, smiling as he looked at the bottle. Then he frowned. "What's this?"

"Chateau Haut-Brion," the waiter said with a slight bow. "The most expensive in the house."

Smith pointed at the label. "This is a '98."

Spare Change

The waiter was perplexed. "Yes."

"This is swill! How dare you!"

The waiter reacted as though there was a lion at his throat. "I assure you—"

"Look, you little shit, you take this bottle of piss back and get me something from a decent year. And tell you boss that if he can't do better, he'll be back flipping hamburgers at McDonald's where he started."

The waiter had turned white. "Yes, sir," the waiter said, backing away and bowing.

Roger watched the scene silently, playing with the silverware. "Do you have many friends, Mr. Smith?"

Smith shrugged. "My colleagues."

"Yes, but are they your *friends*? Can you trust them?"

"Of course."

"Are you *sure*?"

"What's this all about?"

Now it was Roger's turn to smile. "If there's one thing I've learned, is that you guys don't play fair. You change the rules in the middle of the game, just to see how I'll jump."

"That's our specialty."

"What makes you think they aren't changing things right now? Maybe you *are* the next 'it' in this little game of tag."

Smith shook his head. "I'm one of Them. They wouldn't turn on me."

Roger leaned forward. "Wouldn't they? I think that you just might rub people the wrong way. A little too smug. A little too smart. A little too nasty. People don't like that. Not even among Them. And I bet you've made a few enemies who'd like to see you take a fall."

Smith began to smooth his red silk tie as though it was a nervous animal. "It's not going to happen, I'm afraid. You'll just have to find—"

Roger began to sneeze.

It was a violent fit, one after another. The diners were all staring when, with one last explosive "achoo," a computer chip fell out his nose and landed on the white tablecloth.

Smith stared at it with a delightful look of horror.

Roger rose. "Enjoy your meal, Mr. Smith." He stood up and tossed a couple of coins on the tablecloth.

"What's this?" Smith asked. The uncertainty in his voice was very satisfying.

"Spare change," said Roger. "Better get used to it."

The End

Find more great stories, novels, collections, and anthologies at **DigitalFictionPub.com**

Join the Digital Fiction Pub newsletter for **infrequent** updates, new release discounts, and more: **Subscribe at DigitalFictionPub.com**

Copyright

Quickfic Anthology 2 - shorter-Short Speculative Fiction
By Digital Fiction
Quickfic from DigitalFictionPub.com
Executive Editor: Michael A. Wills

These stories are a work of fiction. All of the characters, organizations, and events portrayed in the stories are either the product of the author's imagination, fictitious, or used fictitiously. Any resemblance to actual persons, aliens, dragon, or ghosts, living or dead, would be coincidental and quite remarkable.

Quickfic Anthology 2—by Digital Fiction: Copyright © 2016 by Digital Fiction and the Authors, and published under license by Digital Fiction Publishing Corp., Cover Image: Copyright © Shutterstock ID 221550184 Tithi Luadthong. This version first published in print and electronically: July 2016 by Digital Fiction Publishing Corp., Windsor, Ontario, Canada—Digital Horror/Fantasy/Science Fiction and their logos, and Digital Fiction Publishing Corp and its logo are Trademarks of Digital Fiction Publishing Corp.

All rights reserved, including but not limited to the right to reproduce, copy, and/or archive this book in any form, electronic or otherwise. The scanning, uploading, and/or distribution of this book or the individual stories contained herein via the Internet or any other means without the express written permission of the publisher or author is illegal and punishable by law. This Book may not be copied and re-sold or copied and given away to other people. If you're reading this book and did not purchase it, or it was not purchased for your use, then please purchase your own copy. Purchase only authorized electronic and print editions and do not participate in the piracy of copyrighted materials. Please support and respect the author's rights. Thank you.

Visit us at: **DigitalFictionPub.com**

Made in the USA
Middletown, DE
07 July 2016